Praise for Michael Strelow

Some Assembly Required illuminates the beautiful and mysterious transformation that occurs when we listen carefully to the world.
Scott Nadelson, author of *Between You and Me*

Fascinating, humorous, and wise, *The Greening of Ben Brown* deserves its place on bookshelves along with other Northwest classics.
Craig Lesley, author of *Storm Riders*

The Alyssa
Chronicle

The Alyssa Chronicle

Michael Strelow

OUR STREET
BOOKS

Winchester, UK
Washington, USA

First published by Our Street Books, 2018
Our Street Books is an imprint of John Hunt Publishing Ltd., No. 3 East Street,
Alresford, Hampshire SO24 9EE, UK
office1@jhpbooks.net
www.johnhuntpublishing.com
www.ourstreet-books.com

For distributor details and how to order please visit the 'Ordering' section on our website.

Text copyright: Michael Strelow 2017

ISBN: 978 1 78535 835 7
978 1 78535 836 4 (ebook)
Library of Congress Control Number: 2017951469

A CIP catalogue record for this book is available from the British Library.

Design: Stuart Davies

Printed and bound by CPI Group (UK) Ltd, Croydon, CR0 4YY, UK

We operate a distinctive and ethical publishing philosophy in all areas of our business, from our global network of authors to production and worldwide distribution.

Other Books by Michael Strelow

The Princess Gardener
(Our Street Books: 978-1-78535-674-2)

Some Assembly Required
(Roundfire Books: 978-1-78535-627-8)

The Moby Dick Blues
(Roundfire Books: 978-1-78535-701-5)

Dedicated once again to my cadre of story tellers and story lovers: Ava, Audrey, Lewis, Jackson and Zephyr.

Chapter One

"What do you think you're doing?"

I couldn't tell where the woman's voice was coming from.

"Stop it. Stop it. Stop it."

I stood still, hands by my sides. I was stopping it, I thought, whatever it was. I was stopping everything. After a minute, the voice came again, softer this time.

"You leave my garden alone, and I'll see that you have dried corn each day. Yes. Every day. Silly birds. Fly away now and leave my garden alone."

And then her laugh. And my sigh of relief. She was talking to crows. And I sat right down in the grass on the edge of the woods and laughed at myself.

I could see the garden, the rising crows like black, whirling specks against the sky. And finally, I could see the old woman wagging a finger at the spring clouds.

She was barely taller than the budding flowers around her, her hair sticking out gray against the bright green. She carried a watering can and her apron seemed stuffed with bulky cargo. Her free hand was throwing something over all the parts of her large, square garden.

Then I noticed, far off on the other side, an old man, his head down, slowly making his way across an open patch of ground. And he was making a kind of throwing motion with one hand, too. Maybe he was sowing seeds.

I watched while they moved on opposite sides of the garden like a dance to music only they could hear.

That was the first time I saw them. My mother had mentioned them and where they lived: down the path and through the woods near our farm. And that they seemed to prefer living apart from everyone else—I found out later why.

It was four years ago when I was eight, and old enough to wander the farm by myself for the first time. And usually I had to take my brother, Jake, with me everywhere, but that time he was at the knee of my father learning to mend harness. Jake, I knew, would much rather be in a tree than oiling and sewing leather.

The old couple had whirled into my life. I could never have seen then how large the whirling, how big the circles.

Oh, before I forget, my name is Alyssa and in the years after I first saw the old couple—especially the last two years—my life changed. It changed more than any farm girl's life ever changed, I think. Like the moon becoming the sun. Or like a turtle learning to fly.

It happened quickly, but I'd been ready my whole life. The princess Eugenie—all of us had seen many pictures of her painted for school walls—floated into our classroom as part of some kind of ceremonial blessing of the school, I think. The pictures, it turned out, didn't look exactly like her. But, I did.

Well, not my hair, but just the length. And not my skin color, but that was just my tan from working in the fields. But our eyes were blue with flecks of brown, our noses, in eleven-year-old nose-glory. And then there were her gestures, as soon as she stopped doing the princess waving thing. The way she tugged her earlobe, my ear lobe. The way she smiled to be polite, my smile. The whole business was very, very strange as if someone were playing a kind of mirror joke on both of us. And yet, somehow the clothes, the tan, and the hair length made us seem, to everyone else, just as different as I am from my friend Sheila Susan Brodie. That is, Tuesday from Sunday, cat from dog.

But there we were, the princess looking at me, me looking at her, for what seemed a long, long time. So long that I was sure everyone else would stop their gabbing and catch us looking. But no one did.

She opened her mouth as if she were going to say something to me, then she stopped herself. We stared. All the rest of the children were looking at the Princess, of course. I think my mouth fell open a little bit. But she quickly recovered herself and began to make, what I learned later, were the princess moves that were designed to make everyone comfortable because they were so predictable. Wave, smile—just the right number of teeth showing. I wish I had counted the teeth, because later I had to learn that very same smile, that wave. Fifteen teeth was the right number. Okay, sixteen was acceptable. Any more, I was told, and, well, she explained later, you might eat someone up. And then she had laughed

And that was how it started. I, Alyssa Rankin, the farmer's daughter, would swap places with Eugenie Von Troppen-Goss, from the house of, I guess, both Troppen and Goss. I wasn't sure exactly how that whole name business worked with the royal family. I was sure someone was keeping track of it all. And, as I learned, I was right. But I couldn't know how hugely a big deal it was.

So Eugenie and I swapped places. Well, not at once, of course. We plotted, schemed and practiced. The important thing was that we both liked our new places so much that we hatched plans to keep up the disguise. She loved manure smell, her huge garden plot that fed my whole family, my old creaky bedroom with the window that looked out on woods, my mother and father, and even my younger brother Jake and his monkey-like ways. And I, as I said, I took to the princess stuff like a horse takes to rolling in the dust. I felt as if I had been plucked out of the barn and dropped into a field of fairies, each with a light in her hand on a summer's evening. Which is just like one of the stories I wrote for my little brother, and that was one of my best, if I do say so myself. I specialized in fairies for him, and since he knew absolutely nothing about fairies, I could make up any kind I wanted. What Jake liked was action fairies, so that's what I gave him. When Eugenie and I were working out our little exchange, Jake's likes and dislikes were an important part. There were no romances in his stories, but fairies were not only acceptable, they were required. They could come and go as needed. For example, if a hero needed help, he or she could call in the fairies like a special kind of army, and save the day—*any* day. Jake liked it if I armed the fairies with some kind of fire weapons, so that's why they roamed the evening fields with lit lanterns in their hands.

Jake was more than a minor detail in working out the swap. But once we got the whole thing rolling and Jake decided he liked Eugenie better (or, I claim, just as much) and I managed the castle complications, then we were all set to keep up the swap as long as we liked. So we settled into the new lives we loved. But the problem dealing with the little things is that if you don't take care of the little problems, they become big problems. Like this one.

The castle was buzzing with the news: it was rumored that Arbuckle Beauregard the Third, renowned minister of water and savior of the kingdom's health, was engaged to be married. While that would be of only mild interest in a minor dignitary, Arbuckle had recently, he declared modestly, saved (with some help from Eugenie and me) the kingdom from a polluted water supply and thereby joined his illustrious ancestors, many of whom had been very important in founding the kingdom long ago. Daily I walked corridors with paintings of them. Still no painting of Arbuckle, but that honor would only be a matter of time.

I wanted to take Arbuckle to the old couple's garden, I don't know exactly why. I wanted to plunk him in the grass and have him watch those old folks circle their garden in a dance to music no one else could hear. I felt that the garden might fix what was wrong with him, maybe. But Arbuckle, no matter how big a jerk he was, knew what Eugenie and I had pulled off—the switch. There were very good reasons he wouldn't tell anyone. And for less good reasons, Jake, who knew too, wouldn't tell either.

These days I wander the castle and everyone thinks I am the Princess Eugenie. My own name fades even for me, like something I knew a while ago but can't quite recall now. But the garden, ah. That garden stays right there on top of my brain. The old woman moves there. The old man sows his seeds, the wind pauses for them—holding the world's breath.

The castle had been built over many years and in many pieces so that, it was said, no one person actually knew all the secret passages and rooms and sealed-up dungeons. You could walk down and down into passageways that seemed to be going toward the center of the earth, getting warmer as you went. And it would smell, not bad, but distinct, like nothing else anywhere—not like anything on the farm of my other life, nor any other part of the castle. Then if you kept on walking, suddenly the passage would narrow and stop, blocked by a wall. The smell would be like something burnt long ago and then abandoned, sort of sharp, like a strong cheese, but also like wood smoke carried from far away on a wind.

I am now at the age when I am allowed to go where I want, when I want. That is, outside my duties, outside my shoulds and ought-tos, and outside the plans of my King and Queen father and mother. They assume I am protected by being a princess. In some very important ways, the entire castle staff is here to make sure I get what I want. And I have to admit that being raised on a farm with lots of hard work and then school *only* when the farm work was less in the winter, well, the pampering and smiling and bowing of the castle, kind of went to my head at first. Okay, so maybe some of it stayed there too.

"Watch out for 'princess head,'" Eugenie once advised me. She said it could come on very quickly and my head would swell up and (sort of) explode. And then it would be too late—after the explosion. So, she said, I must try to catch it *before* it happened. Much easier to prevent than to fix. And then she laughed as she always did when she was issuing princess advice, as if the laughter were a way to wash down the bitter medicine.

Eugenie then told the story of a cousin, Bilda, living in a distant castle who had a bad case of "princess head."

Eugenie said, "There she was ordering around the servants, especially older servants who knew everything much better than she did. Bilda stamped her foot before insisting the tea was too cold, or the meat was not cooked right. She raised her voice, then her hand, and finally her scepter with its golden orb. She was ready to strike. Then her father took everything away: her scepter, her title as princess and her power over anyone in the castle. He reduced her to 'stray girl' with an official decree and had it posted everywhere. It said that, until her head grew small again, her sense grew large and she got just a little bit wiser, she would not be in charge of anything. 'Princess head' ruined everything." Eugenie laughed.

I always loved those first sessions when we would breathlessly swap details from our lives so that the other one could take it over. Sometimes we talked both at once and laughed so hard that neither of us could remember exactly what the advice was.

I remember offering, "Put your hand on the horse's rump before you walk behind her, to let her know you're there. Remember horses are prey animals, and they don't like the feeling of anything sneaking up on them."

"Noted," she replied. And then she told me how the curtsy was done only one way, and was not to be done by inventing any old way I felt like doing it at the time. The curtsey was a holy gesture of sorts and the right foot had to know exactly where the left foot was.

And on and on we went in those first days of plotting the switch. It's been two years now and we have become each other. The wonderful lark of it! The giggling at getting away with it for a while! Now both gone. Not only did we get away with it, now it would be very hard to go back. And, of course, that was why — that was *exactly* why — we thought we should do it when Arbuckle's coming wedding was announced.

At first it was all my idea because I hated the thought of what I knew would come. We could swap back, just for a short time, for Arbuckle's wedding when all the relatives of the King and the Queen would come streaming in from the far corners of the kingdom. Some of them hadn't seen Eugenie since she was little. But they would know her and begin tales and stories that I would have no idea about. I'd have to stand and nod and smile. And be completely lost. If Eugenie could just substitute for me for that week of aunts and grand uncles and cousins and second cousins once removed, all would be fine. We thought.

And so in the sweaty old castle, I made for her my list of things to remember. And on the farm, she made her list for me—things we'd have to know to go back temporarily to our old lives.

For example, I loved to cook, so when I first came to the castle I had to insist, and insist again, that the castle cooks let me into the kitchen and let me learn to prepare food—chopping and washing vegetables at first. I already knew these from home on the farm. What I wanted to know was the secret to those tasty sauces served in the dining room, the secrets to perfectly roasted beef cuts we rarely saw at home. And how did the fish get brined and smoked and then sprinkled with dill in the middle of winter? The Queen thought my interest in food something—like the gardening of old—that would go away in time, and that I was just being a headstrong girl insisting on my princess privileges. She was busy; she gave in very quickly, and I was soon in the kitchen reducing an entire bottle of wine to a cup as the base of a fine sauce, and whipping egg yolks into Béarnaise—vinegar, lemon juice, the yolks... So now I had to record it all for Eugenie who had never been interested in cooking when she had lived in the castle.

At the same time, Eugenie recorded all the things she had done differently than I had when I lived on the farm. She had begun a project that required a long list of preparations, though it was exactly the opposite of my new food skills. She operated at the other end of the beast, so to speak. She concocted an elaborate mixture of manures (pig, cow, chicken, rabbit) with some kind of "tea" she brewed that she claimed was alive and quickly broke down the manures into a usable form much faster than before. And the tea-manure "soup" she called it, was going well. Within ten days she could mix it with soil, she said, and use it on her garden or even mix it with the seeds her father (okay, my father) planted in the fields. Plants seemed to grow almost magically on the mixture, like Jack's beanstalk. She had learned to make this soup from the old lady neighbor.

So there we were. Two girls cooking up two very different soups, but, I suspect, out of the same curiosity.

It was all a little confusing for us—the princess had become the farm girl, and I, the farm girl, had become a princess. Now we had to switch it all back for a time.

We decided to meet to compare our lists and notes and to laugh.

The garden the old couple kept was about halfway between us. Their house was nearby, really a large shack, but they had made it comfortable with tight windows, a solid door, and paints they made from berries and roots. Blue and a deep red were their best colors so the house stood at the edge of a wood and looked like elves or faeries must live there. But it was just the two of them, and the old man couldn't see very well. The old woman led him out to the garden each day, and then he seemed to know what to do, as if he could see much better there among his flowers and vegetables. I had known about the couple since I was small, but Eugenie discovered them by accident one afternoon, she said, while picking wildflower seeds to try out in her own garden. The old man had heard her and had beckoned her to come and see his flowers and sit awhile.

So Eugenie had become a regular visitor, and when we were looking for a safe meeting place, she had suggested the garden. And so it was that we met up there, both clutching our lists.

If the old people knew we were princess and princess look-alikes, they didn't let on. And if they knew that one of us was the farm girl from just over the hill, they didn't mention that either. As if they somehow knew that we two with the same face needed space to talk alone, they left us on the beautiful stone bench they had built in the garden among the great nodding heads of dahlias and lacy trim of baby's breath around our feet. We felt like no princess and farm girl had ever felt before, I think. We laughed and pretended we had been dropped into a magic garden where we could talk and have a conversation, each with our own face, our own other self. It was funny and very strange at the same time. Perfectly normal and wildly weird.

At first we took turns talking by holding a small stone. The one holding the stone got to talk by herself because we both had so much to tell and in a rush that we tried to tell it at the same time. Then we passed the stone, and the other one got to talk. This worked at first just to get over the beginning excitement, but soon Eugenie tossed the stone away and we jabbered back and forth like magpies.

She had tales of my brother Jake, who was growing bigger, of course, and knew everything about our whole swap business but was being a great sport about the secret and not demanding anything special. He had not given up his tree swinging, and still she would find him contemplating the world from some leafy perch with his legs dangling over a branch like a serious, philosopher monkey. He would seem to grow still and quiet only when his distance from the ground grew.

On the earth he was in constant motion, appearing here and then there like a pop-up jester who saw the world as his own private joke. In a tree, he was at peace. I thought about how even the idea of Jake in the castle world was, well, simply impossible. No one was allowed to climb trees. No one had the time, especially children, to sit up high and wonder about the world until they felt like climbing down.

I started to tell Eugenie about the new business at court, but very quickly her attention seemed to wander to the flowers as if I had started in on a math lesson of some sort. I had a feeling she had changed her mind about the swap. So I went back to Arbuckle Beauregard the Third and chatted about his rise to the pinnacle of castle social life. I told Eugenie about how, with his forest green outfits, his impromptu lectures on water and the new science of geology, he was at once a newly risen prince among the courtiers and a known pain-in-the butt too.

"He attaches himself to someone and regales them with his new wit and wisdom until their eyes begin to cast about for a polite escape," I said. "But, in general, he remains one of the heroes of the bad-water days — along with me, since I get most of the left-over credit. The girl-credit anyway."

"Well, at least you get some," Eugenie replied. "I get none."

I smiled in sympathy. "His portrait will soon hang with his ancestors, so he is both fulfilled and properly full of himself."

Eugenie warmed to the idea of switching back as we talked, and I carefully moved on to discussing the wedding. I shook my head. "I don't see how I can pull this off with all those relatives coming at the same time." I sighed, waiting for sympathy. But it was slow coming.

"Alyssa," Eugenie said, after a proper wait. "I think you probably could do it. You know, like the smile and wave thing. Just pretend everything's fine and nod. Oh, and maybe say 'um hum,' and then if a grand old lady comes along, touch her arm. They all like that. I have never known it to fail. Touch the arm. Smile. The men like it if you look away and smile. Trust me on this."

I couldn't tell if she was making fun or being serious. It was always hard with her. She'd use her pretending skills and keep a straight face, and then she'd burst out laughing once she knew she had me. But this time she kept the straight face.

I said, "I...I..." It was hard finding the words for my discomfort. "Well, a steady stream of those oldsters, and everybody hearing the answer I give to everybody else, I think that would be the hard part. Now, I can just make up what I don't know and am supposed to know. And then fit it to the person I'm talking to. But trapped! I'd be trapped day after day and the old people would have me there against the wall asking questions, and they'd bite little pieces out of my story and…" I truly was not looking forward to the wedding.

But Eugenie just examined her broken gardening fingernails, lifted her hands for me to see how rough and "country" they had become, and then sighed. "How would these look? How would you look all pink and pretty in my garden? How long would Jake keep quiet? How, how and more how? And also" — she pointed to her face — "there is the matter of freckles." Whichever one of us was outside the most, that was where the freckles flew and alighted on the sunniest face.

Suddenly we weren't both trying to talk at once. I was getting the feeling that my idea of switching back just for the wedding was very far from happening. I had planned to take time to tan a little while Eugenie kept out of the sun for a bit. I had *planned* to mess up my nails while she took better care of hers. I had planned… And so I laid out my plans to her, but Eugenie stayed polite and silent and occasionally shook her head sadly. And very quickly I could see myself in a great and noisy receiving line shaking hands and curtseying and then being besieged by huge flocks of aunts and grand uncles as they flapped their way out of carriages and maybe even out of the sky, too. Who knew? They would be grilling me like a slab of meat. I'd be hung up on the dungeon wall like a…like a….

The steady and earth-loving Eugenie broke my nightmare. "You look like you've lost your final friend. Well, you haven't." She put her hand on my arm in a very princess-like manner. "Let's think about this."

And so we did.

We started the thinking about "this" by talking it through.

I said, "The castle is a different place these days. The soldiers and guards everywhere in the past have been replaced by people talking in rooms about all kinds of things, like clean water, of course. After 'The Great Plague'—that's what they're calling it now—well, after the sickness, Arbuckle was everywhere at once keeping us safe from ourselves. He's a different person now. Oh, and there's the subject of kindness now. I know, I know! Big topic. But somehow the whole business of kindness from the top, from the castle down, has become very important. I'm not exactly sure what they mean by it. The castle buzzes with ideas now: after kindness and water comes how to share wealth. Mostly that comes in the form of making better schools, and then the better education will help spread the wealth around."

I said whatever was on my mind. Eugenie listened as if she were overhearing state secrets. And in a way she was. Somehow the great water plague, the deaths and sickness, had left the kingdom weak in the knees but stronger in the brain. That was all I could figure out.

Then it was Eugenie's turn to talk. "What you say has not appeared in the village yet. The school is making do with very little from the castle. Mostly we pay for our teachers by taking a tenth part of each farmers' market and saving it for the school. Then we wait to see if some money will come from the King and Queen, my mother and father, told me. Well, ha ha, hasn't come yet. But good to know the talk has started. And Jake. Well, he's sort of like a song you can hear in the distance but can't quite make out the words. And now, he's getting muscles. Not little boy muscles, but like the horse has muscles. Like father has muscles. No more roughhouse with him. He's too strong. We'll see how *that* goes. But he has remained, and I hope this continues, a great secret-keeper. Not a peep. He never even lets on in private, no winks and nods. It's like I've always been his sister. Always will be. He likes me, I think, in his own tree-dwelling way."

And then she really warmed to her subject. "There's the garden and farm business, of course." She kind of glowed as she started this matter. "I have found some books and could really use more. Maybe if there was a place that all the books were kept, and you could take some away and then take them back when you were done and then take out some more and…" All this was said in a rush as if she were having a vision of some new world. "The books on farming especially. If we could get more of these—I know there are not too many around. But a place to keep the best ideas for farming around this country. Or maybe borrow from other countries their ideas."

I could see immediately that her excitement was exactly what was needed in the castle and its sudden interest in new ideas. She should be—even for just a little while —where the money was to get those things done. And I should be? But there I felt a tightening in my stomach. We should be back where we started? Really? After we had both come to love our new places?

I spread out the lunch I had brought from the castle: three cheeses, two kinds of bread, the smallest cucumbers and the brightest red grapes. Eugenie had brought the cold water from the farm spring that now ran bright and clean and fresh. We ate, but neither brought up what was becoming clearer: we had to go back to our original lives, even if just for the wedding and then the planning of the new kingdom and its new water and its new joy.

The afternoon wore down to a nub in that sweet garden.

"One last thing," Eugenie said. "I think we have enough time before the wedding to work out a few things besides the fingernails and freckles. If we have to go back, even for a short time, then we should get some good out of all the work." She looked around the garden —big yellow roses here, small red roses there over an arbor—as if she were searching the flowers for a plan. I smiled to myself watching her. When looking for a plan, she always seemed to search a garden or even a patch of dirt for answers. What was she looking for there? I had always worked in our family's garden (yes, *our*, since we both had two families now), and I liked to think I'd worked hard and well. But Eugenie, as if she had sprung up out of the dirt herself, she didn't work in the garden so much as tend it like you would a puppy or new calf. She glided over the garden, while I used to sweat over it. She hummed and chirped while I had grunted at one end of a spade.

And so she cast around the old couple's glowing garden looking for a way to do what we had to do. I waited. She seemed to be checking out the flowers, how they grew, how the leaves waved about, the way the twigs branched. After what seemed to me like a very long time, she took in a deep breath and blew it out, something final, something good.

"How about this? We both look for ways to make each place stronger and healthier."

I knew I'd have to wait for the thought to grow. I couldn't quite see where she was going with this stronger-and-healthier stuff. It seemed at first so, well, so agricultural.

She continued, still looking intently at the flowers as if she were getting some kind of direct message. "We make a chart, each of us, with what we want to see happen on the farms, and in the castle, and then we make a third list. That will be the most important one. That list will be all the things each place can do to help the other place. Sort of like trimming a rose bush. You open up the middle so the air circulates freely and no black spot gets started. You trim away the shoots that cross each other, then keep the first five stems…" And she continued with what I thought was a lesson on rose plants, but in her mind she was clearly somehow laying out our plan for switching back.

I sat fascinated, I'll admit. Her delight in healthy roses was catching, and I couldn't stop myself from smiling — apparently like an idiot.

"Are you even listening to me?" she asked, tapping me on the shoulder. I must have taken my "delighted-idiot" look too far.

"Yes. Sure. Yes, I am. You said trim and air circulation and something about black spot. And I just know you're going to let me know how this will help us plan our returns."

She paused for a moment and looked at me. I could see then how completely she had become a farm girl: take your time, consider your words, give your listener a chance to listen. On the other hand, I had become a fast-talker and damned be anyone who couldn't keep up. My Queen mother called this, "not suffering fools gladly." Apparently I had a lot to learn about "suffering fools," whatever that meant. Whether gladly or not. And also, I had developed this habit just since I'd traded a farmhouse for a castle. I had carefully sought out those around me in the castle who were fast listeners for my fast-talking. That was like dessert to me — the fastness, the quickness of talking and thinking ahead and reacting to someone who was clever: delicious!

Eugenie cocked her head to the side like the horse used to when it didn't understand what I wanted it to do. I cocked my head back at her, and we laughed. I told her that I had got the idea of her plan—three lists, time to think it through, what I thought was needed and how I could help the farm too.

The garden seemed to sigh with Eugenie as she accepted my short version of her flower-based plan. Trim, air, clean, feed and water, I guessed. We would save the kingdom.

There was my problem. My *new* problem. My ever-since-the-switch problem. I had begun to see every side of everything, how complicated everything was, could be. I thought of this as "on the other hand." Everything had an "on the other hand" that was not so clear-cut. And the result was that it was difficult, sometimes, to make a decision. On the farm I didn't have this problem. You couldn't dilly-dally or shillyshally either. Things had to get done and done right away. There was this and there was that and then the other thing too. Boing! Fence was broken. Mend it. Never mind whether the fence was doing what it should be doing and perhaps should be replaced by a better way to keep the cows in. Fix it!

But at the castle, things usually got complicated very quickly. That was the story of the whole bad-water business: nobody could do anything about the sickness from the water because everybody was consulting someone else, and they in turn... Well, too much thinking and not enough doing. But the thinking part, I had to admit, became very interesting, even when it kept any solution to the problem flapping off there in the blue sky like any old butterfly that wouldn't land.

Eugenie and I waited in the garden until the very last minute. The sun was dropping; we'd be missed at home and castle. The old woman appeared and asked if we wouldn't like something to eat, and said she had some cookies. But we had to hurry. We were two girls with a (sort of) plan.

We would have to think, list, think some more. Plot the switch. The old man, as we were leaving, appeared at the edge of his garden and waved goodbye to us. I wondered if he could somehow see when he was in the garden but not when he was out of it.

Chapter Two

I returned to the castle full of a combination of excitement and, I'll admit, fear. I had the castle routine down pretty well, the shuffle and slide of the whole thing, the way lots of new things have when all is exciting and first-time. I felt right away that I was part of an ancient dance and everyone else knew the steps: where I moved, who I talked to, when I lined up to receive important people. And the portraits on the walls of important people from the past, these were only a few, and not always the most important, of the dance makers.

Some days I wanted to make clicking noises and move like a doll caught in a wind-up machine. I never did it, but I wanted to paint my eyes like a china doll, move my hands stiffly, squeak my shoes as I went through the movements. Somehow, it was good just to pretend to do it, just think about it. That helped me not actually do it, I think. I understood very soon why Eugenie had wanted out. But also, just as soon, I felt the opposite, the old on-the-other-hand. The importance of the dance and my part in it. The princess part.

And, I have to admit that this part got away from me a little—the deadly princess-head; I felt that I had been meant to be a princess all my life. I wanted something more than the warm side of a cow at milking time, the dull slowness of a schoolroom with all ages being taught at once. The tutors, Eugenie's tutors, had picked me up right where she left off. Not one of them suspected a thing because Eugenie, who hadn't much cared for the whole tutor business, had told me clearly where she was in each subject. If any of them noticed that I was suddenly a much more eager student, they didn't say a word.

So, I had scrambled a little at the beginning of the math, but quickly got the idea. I soon found I wanted more, way more than the tutor was scheduled to give me. His teaching had what I called the princess-limit—just enough math to be useful to a young woman with royal duties. So when soon after returning to the castle after my talk with Eugenie, he tried to call off our sessions just when they got interesting, we had, well, let's call it a discussion. I'm not proud of my imperiousness—that was the word I learned later, the word used for a princess too big for her britches.

Mr. Andors had been wrapping up our number discussion. "And so these addings and subtractings and multiplyings and dividings, these you will grow comfortable with as you see their usefulness. I think that concludes our..."

"But wait," I insisted. "What about how the numbers work? When do we get to the way they really work? What about, for example, if we pile up the numbers in groups then set up a way the groups can...what? I don't know the right words. Can...can talk with each other. That's not right, but certainly the number groups can be piled in a way that they change in value if you... Oh, I can think of what I want to say, but I don't know the right words. Can we learn how to talk about what numbers can do...be?... when the groups are put together in a way so that..."

Mr. Andors started to pack up his papers. He wasn't listening. He thought his job was done. It was no excuse, of course, but his packing up, his ignoring what I thought was very interesting and exciting, *that* set me off. Okay, made me crazy.

"Stop it," I yelled. "Stop, stop, stop that fiddling and listen." Oh, this was not going to turn out well, but I couldn't seem to help myself. What had crossed my mind for just a second was the old lady yelling at the crows in her garden. Then the spoiled-brat imperiousness had ahold of me fiercely. "You put those papers down right now and tell me what I want to know!" I stomped my foot. "You want to just walk away from this lesson right when it gets interesting. Well, no! You *will* continue, right now. You *will* tell me what is known about groups and how they..."

Mr. Andors stood perfectly still with his papers in hand, frozen by my barrage of princess insistence. His job, I was sure, flashed in front of his eyes. The displeasure of the princess was the displeasure of the King. And the King's anger was slow to come but legendary in consequences. I could see his fear, but I couldn't stop myself. The poor man, I thought. But then his eyes grew bigger and bigger. I could see what he was thinking. Would the princess leap at him like a lioness? Was his life at the castle about to be finished? My princess snit grew. Though he showed all the signs of giving in to my demands, I couldn't slow myself down.

"The. Groups. Of. Numbers. Are." I insulted his intelligence, his manhood, his station as a teacher. As if speaking to child, I dragged out each word, each syllable. Not a child. A fool! I spoke to him as if he were an idiot. Poor Mr. Andors just stood there and took it. And I would have gotten away with my childish rant if my mother hadn't been standing just outside the door listening. She came in at that exact moment when I was going to make an imperious fool of myself, and she dismissed Mr. Andors. Then she sat me down, and let me have it, slowly at first, then picking up speed. It was what I deserved. A good talking to.

Besides the vocabulary of the talking to, there was the time, while I listened to her, for me to cool down and rethink what had made me so mad. The mother-talk flowed and ebbed, as those things did. Valuable not only

The Alyssa Chronicle

for what was said but for the whole opportunity for me to review my actions.

But what I thought about later was more interesting to me. Okay, I was wrong and imperious. Okay, I could have made my request without insulting the man, the teacher, the subject of the kingdom. And, okay, I could have taken the time to patiently pursue my goal of more education. All those okays. But what had made me so crazy in the first place? That was worth thinking about.

Those groupings of numbers and their operations, the possibilities of substituting names for the groups and then collecting them in a kind of sentence that would describe something changing—a surface or something slowing down or speeding up—that idea grabbed me as fiercely as my spoiled-brat rant. I don't really know why the number business grabbed me so. It was all sort of a gooey mess in my head, all these things I didn't understand coming together in the example of number groups. It wasn't actually the math; it was all the things I wanted to know but wasn't being given a chance to know. Equally fierce were my outrages. I sat alone in my room licking my wounds from the talking-to, and I held up my two hands like a scale weighing the outrages. Bad behavior on the right. Getting my curiosity shut off on the left. Up and down I shifted the scale. Which one weighed the most? Humm. Tip the scale. Fiddle the results. And I found my curiosity heavier, more valuable, than my good behavior. I knew I shouldn't. I certainly owed Mr. Andors an apology, and he would get one, I promised myself. But there it was! What I wanted to know easily outweighed my rudeness.

When a horse became anxious or impatient, it chomped on the bit and twirled it around in its mouth, that horse tongue going round and round. So I recognized my own chomping. I was ready to go. But where? To where the math

22

went—the math I wasn't getting? To where the diplomats went after they left the public rooms and went away to talk about things too secret for the rest of us? I wanted it all, but I was heading back to the farm instead. These two things pulled at me. I'd let Eugenie handle Arbuckle's wedding. Then I'd fake the farm things—easy. Pretty soon I'd be back at the castle looking for more than was allotted a mere princess—chomping. I could see trouble coming, but there wasn't a thing I could do about it.

Eugenie and I thought we had plenty of time to think and make lists and talk and plan. We didn't. Arbuckle Pemberton The Third had announced his wedding a year away, but then some traveling important people combined with some other schedule problem changed everything. It seemed that, more important than the wedding itself, was who attended. If the right people were there, the wedding would be a successful event. Not enough of the right people, for whatever reason, and the wedding would be nothing, and historians would leave that page blank. Arbuckle, of course, knew how that worked. He had recently added his own name to the history books by becoming the savior of the kingdom helped (well, he was really the one who "helped") by two girls. And those two girls (that was Eugenie and me) decided that continuing their game of changing places was more important than getting the proper credit for their discovery of the bad water.

So, the wedding was suddenly just six weeks away, the new date perfect for many of the most important people who would attend. And the people at court who read the favor of the moon and stars, they also found the new date to be much better than the old date. The flowers, which were to be grown especially for the event, now had to be found somewhere in the countryside. Every farm and ditch would have to be scoured and then picked clean. The food for the feast was to have been gathered on the hoof and claw and paw—however it moved—and then fattened for the guests' meals. Now it would have to be hunted and bargained for. Scouting parties were readied. The castle suddenly became a tornado of cleaning and patching. Castles, I had learned, are fragile things. They came apart easily and had to be fixed constantly. Those great blocks of stone sat on top of each other reluctantly, it turned out. They had to be persuaded to stay there by many workers carrying hods of cement and brick and yards of iron wire. The roof, the *many* roofs, were the most fragile. The way it was talked about in the castle, it seemed to me as if things came in the night and made off with the slate tiles from the roof. I could never quite figure out how it happened, but slabs of gray slate somehow flew up into the air and disappeared at night so that in the morning the only thing left on the ground below was a pile of grayish dust. Then workers had to rope themselves together and scramble across the slippery slopes putting new slate in place.

It was all a never-ending process that became like a circus as the wedding date drew near. Acrobats everywhere! Daring young men on the roof swinging from peak to peak. And inside, more daredevils scaling the walls to clean the corners and patch the stones. The wall hangings came down and were hauled to the creeks to be bathed and scrubbed. Every musician in the country was tempted into the castle with promises of money and food and then captured there and set to practice for the festivities. Tents went up around the outside walls for the carriers and cleaners and bringers and takers. Out went the garbage. In came the fresh supplies of cloth and sharp knives and gold paint. The castle was becoming a huge circus and growing bigger every day.

So Eugenie and I found ourselves hurrying up our plans. Her fingernails had to be groomed, her freckles faded. My fair skin needed tanning and at least a few callouses cultivated for my hands. Think that was easy? Just the callouses alone cost me hours a day of doing something that was like work. Princesses don't work. At least not that way. So I had to find some way toughen my hands. I found it in my favorite place—the kitchen.

Our grand scheme for setting everything right for the switch back had now become a scramble to get just the obvious stuff right. Never mind the list of what to know, who was new, which friends thought what. We'd have to fake that after all. Eugenie even asked if we shouldn't maybe perhaps, forget about the switch back and just let me pretend my way through the reception line. But to me, the whole business of going back for a while was growing more and more attractive. I felt that my math-class outrage would only be the beginning of things going wrong, and maybe going back to the farm for a while would help me be a nicer princess, be a better daughter to the Queen. So we decided to plunge right in and see what happened.

Here's what happened. The old man's garden was stolen— I'm sure that's the right word even though the wedding master used the word "appropriated." His people came and put up signs that the flowers now belonged to the castle, and he thanked the old couple for their contribution to the glorious wedding of you-know-who. Yes, Arbuckle Pemberton—old number three. The sign continued that, from now on, "care of the flowers would be in the hands of official representatives of the nation. All others would be considered trespassers on the King's property." Apparently this "appropriation" went on everywhere in the kingdom, but for Eugenie and me, it was our garden too. And for Eugenie especially, gardens all over the kingdom were under her personal care.

What started out small, close to the castle, grew terrible and large. The small flower gardens like the old man's got "stolen" and then the wedding organizers from the castle, under someone's order, reached out like some mean octopus all around the kingdom and declared every flower garden they could find to be the "King's property." The sign posted at each garden actually said that "the flowers and some food stuffs of this garden" were now subject to the King's declaration number 4038, section II: "What is deemed necessary for the proper functioning of the kingdom may, in an emergency, be declared the sole property of the King's will."

Here's what Eugenie wrote me in a letter.

You wouldn't believe it, Alyssa. At first one lone rider came to the house and without asking, inspected our (my) garden and then suddenly there were twelve other riders—with arms—who declared my garden the property of the King's whim. I, of course, knew exactly what was going on. Their horses stomped and steamed in the barnyard, the men dismounted and stood around rigidly. I wanted to tell them who I was and kick their behinds down the road as far as the creek and then kick them into the creek. But, of course, I didn't. I just stood there fuming while that sergeant oaf who I've known as a goofball for many years, read out the decree claiming my garden, my hard work, the property of my own father! I think steam came out of my ears. I think knives flew out of my eyes. I knew exactly where the flowers would go and what food would be raided from my garden (I have been to royal weddings before, and I knew the waste, too), and worst of all, I knew for whom all this would be done; well, I nearly turned inside out with rage. And, yes, did nothing.

Arbuckle Pemberton the Third, indeed! Until very recently a clownish fop in a silly-suit.

I took a deep breath reading this. I could just see Eugenie standing there undone and wanting all her princess-power back, even if just for ten minutes while she set the world right. Then she would want to fade back into being a gardener, of course. I read on.

In a minute I realized that these men were not the ones responsible for this looting business. Maybe not even my father and mother. Maybe, almost certainly, not Arbuckle himself. The whole sad looting scheme probably started with some bright fellow or lady who had to come up with a wedding fit for the important guests, but didn't have the normal amount of time to do it. And so, the robbery. The plain insolent thievery of it! They would make the wedding work by stealing the labor of every plant-loving gardener for many miles around. What a wrong! A crime!

And here followed a list of words like crime, sin, wrong, etc., that Eugenie used to let out her anger on the poor page. She couldn't attack the King's men; she couldn't turn the air blue with her anger. But she could scorch the page with words. And she did. Here's how she ended.

Well, Alyssa, that at least feels better, telling you. You know I talked to you about princess-head when we were going to change places. Told you not to get one. Told you what happens. But I found myself growing fiercer and fiercer in that direction as if all the world were wrong and I were right. And I'd stomp my foot and bellow in the world's ear and tell them all to go to their rooms and not come out until they got right in the head. Of course, I recognized princess-head happening to me, but, you know, I think if you are right, sometimes maybe princess-headedness is just the right thing. Move over world, I'm going to fix you now! Oh, Alyssa, I watched those men circle my garden and tie a giant ribbon around it and declare it the King's property, and I cried inside. I wouldn't give them the satisfaction of crying on the outside. The oaf pounded in a stake with the sign attached, and it was done. Thirteen horses pooped, it seemed, at the same time filling our barnyard. And the men rode off having left manure everywhere, only some of it from their horses. We have to hurry up our plans to switch back. Make lists of what I should know. Think of everything! Come prepared to do this quickly. I suddenly have the itch to walk the halls of the castle with my nose in the air, ordering people around and being a thorn in the side of, well, everybody!

Uh oh, I thought as I finished reading. This may be the end of everything: our new lives we loved, our delicious new lives. I imagined Eugenie wild through the castle like a fire, her flames shooting here and there, chasing the court before her and burning the place down with her rage. I also realized that Eugenie would cool off some as we switched back, that she knew that whatever was to be done, it had to be done with some kind of grace or we'd have the whole swapped-lives thing blow up in our faces.

I thought I could hear her seething even at this distance from the farm. She'd walk out in the morning and see the King's pen around her garden, the garden she was expected to tend each day with water and weeding, just so they could come and pick the flowers for the wedding. And in case they needed beet greens and young peas, they'd pick those too and move on like so many locusts. I had to admit, though, there was a part of me that liked the confusion of what I thought was coming. The explosion of people, the chasing around, the blaming. It would all be very exciting even if it was dangerous. I asked myself, would the pure excitement of it make all the damage worthwhile? Alas, I knew myself. It would. It would! That same curious part of me didn't give a fig what kind of mess got made as long as it was interesting.

Sometimes, I confess, I used to make a mess of life if I got a little bored. I'd see how long Jake could take kidding before he erupted and swung off into a tree somewhere. Or I'd chase the heifers and try to ride them, though I knew not to. To see if I would get caught? I really don't know why. But something in my life on the farm made me do what I never did in my castle life. That was probably why I didn't want to risk losing the change. The princess business kept getting more complicated. I liked that.

Chapter Three

The wedding was less than a month away, and if we were going to change places, we knew it would have to be soon. I had done my part: cultivated freckles with my face in the sun as often as possible (for a princess), then covered the freckles with waxy makeup so I could reveal them later. I would have to crack my nails and split hair ends right before the switch. Eugenie's hair had lightened from so much sun. She had to protect her hands any way she could. The plan was to deal with her freckles when the time came. And it came; I got an urgent note from her.

It said, NOW.

We met in the old couple's garden, ducked under the confining ribbon, and sat on their fine bench.

Eugenie was a little out of breath as if she'd run all the way, so we sat a while not talking. She started out twice as if looking for the right direction. "I wanted to... Just wait a minute. We have to get going pretty soon. If we don't, they'll take everything. I have to stop them."

She was talking about flowers, but it could have been children or babies or the eyes from our heads. Eugenie was glowing like the great yellow dahlias just behind her.

"Everywhere they're going to take the flowers from people's gardens just because *they* messed up the wedding planning." She was outraged. Her blue eyes—*our* blue eyes—big as saucers. Her outrage was my outrage. Her letter had come to life.

"What can we do?" I asked.

"Arbuckle could stop it. And certainly the King and Queen! *You* could stop it."

The garden ticked and sighed around us, like voices too

far away to hear. The old couple were nowhere in sight. But the flowers were their ears and eyes it seemed to me, somehow including them in our plans. We plotted with petals and stems, with roots and leaves. The thought made me almost giggle.

Trying to be serious, I said, "If I can stop it, you can stop it. Okay, what's your plan?"

And here we hurried up all of the steps of our scheme to switch back. I had a bad feeling that hurrying this up was going to cause problems. But there we were, surrounded by flowers, about to risk everything to save the flowers, and the flowers did nothing but wave at us when a breeze came up. I didn't know what I expected, maybe a thank you. Maybe a delegation from the daisies or a representative from the zinnias to stand up for themselves. I always got silly when I couldn't guess what was going to happen, when I got nervous. I think that silly was my way to take the uncertainty out of things. Silly was a great calmer for me. I told Eugenie about my hope that the flowers would somehow let us know their gratitude. Even just one squeaky thanks from those little purple flowers—what were they?—that grew like bunches of grapes. But she was too deep in her plotting thought to do much more than nod. Yeah, yeah, she seemed to say. Let's get some work done here.

And so we did. Everything we had planned got turned into the quick version so we could begin action: freckles, fingernails, hair, callouses, updates of family and castle activities and Jake and Arbuckle information. Those two would certainly be onto the re-switch immediately and would want to know why. Those two again, just like before when we first switched. We'd have to navigate around them. They both knew, of course, but they both might balk at the strangeness of our plans and mess us up plenty.

We decided that evening would be the best time to switch back: people were tired, not paying attention; we'd only have to pretend for a few hours then go to bed, and the next morning, things-as-usual would give us a running start at the new day. We talked long about this—morning versus evening for the switch. What finally sold us both on evening was the light. Firelight was the most forgiving, we decided. Things by firelight always seemed fine. The harsh morning light would show flaws and errors. We returned—me to the castle, she to the farm—with our hurry-up plans jangling in our heads.

Two days later, we set out from two directions to meet again in the garden. By the evening light we could see the old couple's house was dark too; they had gone to bed early, as they always did. Eugenie and I exchanged clothes, whispered goodbye and good luck and headed back to where we had started in life, both of us leaving our new life reluctantly.

At the farmhouse, I crept up to my bed while the rest slept. At the castle, I thought Eugenie would have more problems—guards, people who always seemed to be wandering the halls at night, and the maids, who were always checking to see that she was safe or if she wanted something. I smiled to myself as I slipped between my old, familiar bedcovers, turned to the window as I used to, and smelled the woods and then the barn as the breeze shifted. I could hear the crickets and now and then night-bird music that decorated the dark. It seemed I had just put my head down when it was light.

I could hear my mother below in the kitchen. My father was lighting the fire. I took a deep breath and jumped right back into my old life armed, for the first few minutes anyway, with the information Eugenie had given me about the collapse of a roof at the market. Who was hurt, who was responsible, what was going to be done? My mother, without missing a beat, continued the conversation she had begun with Eugenie the day before. I acted my part. The change was perfect. I felt I had landed on my feet. And running. Off to the barn after breakfast to do the old familiar chores. Here I was, a princess with a pitchfork mucking out the stalls, milking the cows, humming my old songs.

Jake entered. I had my back to him, my forehead against the cow.

"Hi, Alyssa."

"Hi, Jake."

That was how much it took for him to make the discovery.

"Welcome back," he said, as if he had been in on the whole thing.

I thought I had better play it out a little longer. "Whatever do you mean? Back to the barn? I was here yesterday. Same old cow. Same old pail."

"Yeah. Got ya. Mum's the word."

And that was the whole thing? I would like to report that he slowly figured it out, and that there was great drama, the secret finally coming out. But no. Bang, just like that. He was onto us. And the amazing thing was that he didn't seem to care one way or the other. I'm still not sure what he saw or sensed. He was like an old dog that had only to sniff the air twice to get the truth. He was behind me! He couldn't see my face. What could it have been? But I was not going to bring it up as long as he was willing to go along and let live. And that left a nagging feeling in the back of my brain that somehow, somewhere he'd want something in exchange for his good will. You know, as if he had it all in the bank like money, and he'd just wait to take it out. Rascal. I loved him dearly, but he was a rascal—a good rascal.

And so the day went on. My mother and father were busy with the farm. I knew how to fit in, and the return was seamless, sort of.

"Lyssie," my mother said to me later. She was the only one who shortened my name this way. It was the badge of her being my mother. "Please keep the garden up. I know how angry you were when the King's men said it belonged to the castle now. But we don't want trouble with them. Let's think of it as a gift. A gift so we can live in peace." She patted my back to calm me.

Eugenie is much more a foot-stomper than I am. She told me she'd threatened to destroy her flowers before letting the castle take them. Our mother had promised to discuss it with our father, and they would talk to her about it. Eugenie told me she wanted to eat all the vegetables, pick all the flowers and leave the King (her father, remember) nothing but a patch of bare ground. And, she raved that she planned to leave her father's men an additional prize of a big pile of manure right in the middle. Our parents would not take kindly to the idea of getting crosswise with the King.

I mumbled to my mother something about doing what I could to keep the peace. But I knew that Eugenie, would be roaring through the castle, and would be the one really doing what had to be done. From the castle she would have a big stick to wave. On the farm, I thought it best to let things alone in the meantime.

I went to tend the King's garden, get dirt under my fingernails and crack one or two, begin work on a few callouses, get acquainted with Eugenie's new fertilizer mix, and say hello to the animals. Jake had swung up into some high perch out of sight. He always did his chores quickly so that he was free to do whatever he did up in trees. What a strange and wonderful brother! He was like a monkey in a people suit.

Eugenie was, I imagined, finding her way around the castle. I hoped she was taking her time, as I was doing, and was working her way back into the swing of things there. The scurry of preparations for Arbuckle's wedding was, I knew, underway. There were more people in the castle than ever before. I hoped she was greeting everyone who greeted her and making her way into the kitchen where I had spent a lot of time learning the sauces. I thought of my kitchen time as graduating from the garden. I began thinking about vegetables in a new way. A beet in my farm-world would poke up out of the ground, then be pulled up, washed off and boiled. Of course, we'd eat the leaves too. But in the castle kitchen, the beet was slow roasted or pickled or carved into a blood-red flower to decorate the meat that had to be brought to the table like a work of art. I knew immediately I wanted to learn these mysteries. And, as I said, my Queen mother indulged me, thinking my interest, like Eugenie's dirt fascination, would run its course, and I would get on with the princess stuff.

The farm garden—Eugenie's garden—was already aglow with health. The mixture she had invented—her super soup, she called it—was obviously doing its job. The beans were twining up the trellises she'd made, four poles tied together at the top. Tendrils waved in space feeling for the next grip to reach for the sun. Her flowers were brilliant: large dahlias in yellow and red and one mixture of the two, blue larkspurs she had grown from wild seed, delphiniums in another blue, then rows of zinnias and dianthus and geraniums she had spaced for red-orange-pink splotches. Looking at them, I could just see Eugenie's saucer eyes growing larger with anger when she'd told me about the "looting" of her garden.

She had generations of plants with some just started and some mature and flowering so that she'd have flowers to cut right through the first frost. Her cosmos, fall flowers, were just beginning, hiding among the towering summer blooms. Eventually they'd get leggy and fill the space with dazzling pink. I think she kept the garden to have bright colors around.

Our farm clothes were all homespun grays and browns of the original yarns. All the brightly colored clothes of the castle were bright only until they were washed. Then, with the first washing, the dyes ran in rainbow streams and the clothes were dull with barely a hint of their original color. I was stunned when I found out that most clothes were worn once by the ladies and then thrown out and replaced. There was a second life of sorts as the clothes trickled down the social ladder to maids and others where they were remade and worn with all the juicy colors gone.

I sighed some over the garden wondering what to do. The food as well as the flowers would be looted—in the future, of course. Nobody knew how much of the food would be taken; but we all knew the flowers were marked for Arbuckle's marriage. About every four or five days a rider would come from the castle and simply trot into the farm yard, look at the garden and then ride off. I guessed he was checking that we didn't pick our flowers or, worse yet, not water and tend them.

It wasn't long before I heard, *we all heard*, that a farm wife two valleys over had simply abandoned her flower garden after it had been taken. No water, no fertilizer, not staking up the heavy flower heads. Soldiers came and she was dragged from the house and put to work replanting the garden while the farmer and her children stood by. She wasn't injured, but the King's men stayed to make sure that she planted a new garden and, well into the evening, she was released to go and cook for her family. From what I knew of the castle types, some self-appointed person had decided on this punishment to make an example of her. The garden, of course, would not give the wedding flowers. But the message was clear: all the flowers belonged to the King.

I couldn't help myself. I immediately began to think about blowing up the whole Arbuckle wedding. It was fun to think that Eugenie and I could raise a "garden army" that would pick all the flowers before the wedding and feed them all to the livestock. Wouldn't that be hilarious! We'd appear together, both dressed as the princess as if princess-power had suddenly doubled and had taken over the country. We'd frog-march hapless Arbuckle out in front of his intended bride and shame him for letting the King's men commit flower mayhem in his name. We'd insist that only vegetables could decorate his wedding. There would be cauliflower centerpieces with sprigs of rosemary sticking out. Broccoli florets would be arranged like tiny forests with little brown mushrooms scattered below. Beets would be carved into red accents here and there. Onions and leeks and garlic bulbs would hang from poles in braided glory.

I mused to myself about this: *You know who would like this vision? Eugenie, that's who. She'd chime in her contribution and we would laugh and laugh. But, of course, we really wouldn't risk everything on a lark like that. Would we? Bring the whole charade of the last year to a crumpled pile on the castle floor? No, no no no. Eugenie give up what she had longed for her whole life? Me give up what was just getting very interesting for me — the life of court intrigue in the halls of power? Still, how much fun would it be for a short while? A royal wedding with wheat sheaves tied up in little pointy triangles. Pumpkins—oh, joy, where do I begin? Heads with carved faces lit up in fools' grins. Stacked into mazes with secret passageways. At this point, we'd have to consult with Jake for the high tree decorations, the stalks to hang from trees to blow in the wind. The strings of bean stalks and paw-paws and maple leaves draped high above the festive vegetable-festooned tables.*

It was fun imagining it all. I didn't even mention my musings to Eugenie. I would find out very soon after that day what she was up to at the castle as we met again in the old man's garden. He and the old lady were nowhere to be seen. But I noticed immediately—my newly acquired princess sensibilities—that the bench had been thoroughly cleaned off for us.

Chapter Four

Things had changed since Eugenie had walked the castle halls as a princess. She told me she'd found herself a stranger, but a stranger who was required to nod and greet her way along the hallways. Corrine, her old nanny and then protocol chief, had become some kind of main organizer for Arbuckle's wedding. She plowed the hallways issuing orders. Eugenie wondered if she had been the source of the flower-looting scheme. I told her I didn't know.

Eugenie retold the story of when she was young, chasing Corrine around the garden with muddy hands threatening Corrine's white apron; how powerful Eugenie felt the mud must be if it could scare this full-grown woman into running away from her. She said that maybe, just maybe, that was the first time she realized the power of dirt that would occupy her mind the rest of her days.

I said, "The flower business seems to have been one of those things where somebody suggested something and then a bunch of other people jump on the bandwagon. It came from nowhere and then somebody said, 'of course,' and then somebody else patted that one on the back and it grew from there. The talk was about how important this wedding was because our kingdom would act as a lesson in good conduct for all the visitors. It seems no one was thinking anything except the impression we'd make on our neighbors. No one, I guess, thought about the gardeners working every day to have beautiful flowers. I heard an old advisor mention that he believed all the flower growers would be delighted to add their bounty to the kingdom's great day. He said we'd show our neighbors how to do it. We would teach them about water and how great people should live. And then, you know, on and on. Blah, blah.

But he was serious! He had no, what should we call it? No sympathy. It was like he had a hard time even imagining what it was like to actually be someone else."

Eugenie sighed. "And we would begin this lesson by stealing all the flowers in the kingdom from the people who grew them! How dumb has this become?" Little devils and flying knives didn't really come out of her eyes, but it certainly seemed like they could. She had been back in the castle for only a short time and wanted to try out some ideas on me before she attacked the wedding plans. I didn't dare tell her my imagined scheme where we would feed all the flowers to the livestock and then impose vegetable decorations on Arbuckle's festivities. She just might jump on the idea and insist we do it.

She seemed to calm down a little, and said, "I need some time with you to keep my plans reasonable. I know that."

Our time on the bench, the magically clean bench I might add, was like adding up our two brains, our two versions of one face but two selves so that we could rise up into the sky like a big, thinking bird. Or that was my version, anyway. Eugenie's version was just caution. But hurry-up caution because the time was getting tighter each day. We only had time to try one thing, and then the wedding would be upon us, and it would be too late. That is, unless we brought the livestock *to* the wedding and let it roam and eat the flowers... I reined in my imagination like an unruly horse.

I didn't notice it until Eugenie-the-gardener pointed it out, but all around us the flowers were fresh and new. She said there were always flowers fading and being replaced by new buds. Most plants had some kind of cycle. But here in the old man's garden, the old woman's too, all the flowers were full and beautiful. "It's not natural," she said, and we both laughed because it was the very thing

Arbuckle had said about the two of us once he found out our secret. It's not natural. You bet.

Then a stranger thing happened.

The old lady appeared in the doorway of the pretty cottage, with its red berry-colored shingles, and the deep blue of the door. She stood, a tidy apron around her waist, her hair gray and alive as if birds lived in there. She had her hands on her hips and seemed to be surveying her garden and trees and us. The old man was nowhere to be seen.

After a minute, she waved over the whole scene as if blessing us all and then turned and went into the house. But very soon she came out again carrying a watering can. She tipped it to sprinkle the flowers in the window boxes around the house, but it seemed from where we were that nothing came out of the can. Still, she continued to water as if the can could never run out: first the vegetable garden, followed by several small trees at the edge of her apple orchard, and then she turned to the garden where we sat.

Eugenie said that it was time for us to go. I wanted to stay and watch the pretend watering or whatever it was. But Eugenie insisted and tugged my arm. She said we should take the path back to the farmhouse, and then she would go back to the castle through the woods. But I wanted to watch the old lady a little longer. The inexhaustible watering can still poured out something invisible.

"She taught me the secret for making my fertilizer soup," Eugenie said, as if what we were watching was perfectly normal.

"But there's nothing coming out of the spout. Is she just pretending to water?"

"It looks that way, doesn't it? But I think something must be coming out. Look how carefully she waters each plant. The big plants get more. The small ones get less time. So she must think she's doing something. That's what I see. She's certainly saying something too, words we can't hear. Once I was just behind a tree watching, and she really wasn't saying anything out loud. But the watering and the talking must be something because, look! The plants certainly are doing well."

We watched from where the paths went separate ways. The old lady continued her rounds, and I knew it must be just that the light was changing, you know, the way it changes toward evening when the sun gets low. But the plants seemed to light up, and the colors got brighter after she watered them. She made a path around the garden leaving a glowing trail like a magic snail. Eugenie held up her hand when I started to speak. "I know," she said. "Watch."

And the old lady finished her rounds, the sun slid into the trees, and the entire garden was a kind of fire in the clearing. I think I held my breath because suddenly I found myself gasping for air as a sign for the world to get back to normal.

Eugenie finally said, "There is some part of what she does that I think I will never understand. I was taking a walk one afternoon a long time ago, when I saw this for the first time. And there's one more thing—well, I think there are *many* more things, really—but one more thing for now. The people from the castle came to put the ribbon around her garden. You know, the one that says these now belong to the King. And the workers tried to walk across the garden but somehow couldn't. They could put the ribbon *around* it all right. But they couldn't seem to get into it. I think it will be interesting when they come to pick these flowers for the wedding. I want to be here to watch. But maybe that will be you this time. You have to watch carefully and tell me everything."

The old lady circled back toward the house but stopped

to admire her handiwork. She set down the watering can and wiggled her fingers as if greeting a small brown bird that had flown down from a tree. I had to be getting back home. I didn't know what to think about what I'd seen or what Eugenie had just told me. I had to go. We would talk next time.

I had known about this old couple all my life. My parents said they preferred to live by themselves, and that I should leave them be. My father said only to talk to them if they asked me something. I knew that Jake would climb the trees in the woods just outside their clearing, and that he would watch and watch. I asked him what he saw, what was so interesting. He only said that he didn't know why, but he liked to watch their house and garden from high in a tree. It made him, and these were his exact words, "feel like I'm just two eyeballs in the tree." I asked him what he meant, and he said that he sometimes felt as if he had disappeared and was only the looking part and nothing else. And the further I pressed him to explain, the more words came out of his mouth that sounded like pure nonsense. The harder he tried to explain, the worse it got. I gave up. But it was Eugenie in her comparatively short time in my place, who had seen the strange power of the old couple—the nearly blind man who could see without his eyes, the old lady who pretended to water with water no one could see. Personally, I preferred things like my experiment with mice. I could write down what I saw, make up my mind, and then see what I had found out. The light, the invisible water, the finger wiggling—these confused me.

But not Eugenie. Before she left to go back to the castle, she said, "Those people are not what they seem. I mean, I can feel the difference. Can't you?" Well, I couldn't. I saw what I saw, but there was probably a good explanation for all of it. We were too far away to see the water coming out; she was only giving a little to each plant, so the water lasted a long time; the evening light is always a little strange—everyday! Eugenie could see that I wasn't ready to believe what she called "the difference." I guess my face showed it pretty clearly.

"Okay. You don't see what I see," Eugenie said.

"I think since I was raised on a farm, I'm ready to explain real things even when they seem strange. We had a calf once with six legs. No weirdness. It just happens sometimes. There was a crow that came to live in the barn and it talked. It said 'Alyssa,' and 'June.' *My name and a cow's* it called out every day for about three months, and then it was gone."

Eugenie rolled her eyes, waved at me and was off up the road back to the castle. I worked my way through the small woods and out into our field. I was feeling a little bad about not going along with Eugenie's wonder at the power of the old woman. I could have been better about my friend's excitement. It was later I found out how right she was.

The big storms came every few years, so everyone on farms knew what to do. If the field was full of ripe wheat, you tried to get it cut as soon as possible. If the wheat wasn't ripe, there was nothing to do but shrug your shoulders, pick your teeth and wait for the long stalks to get flattened. Lots of wheat would be lost after the storm flattened the field, but what could you do? My father always said you could pray. Or you could get mad at the sky or you could go do something else. That was where his shrug would come in as he set off to mend fences.

The clouds would build in the west like great gray giants

peeking over the horizon. And then another one would peek over the top of the first and then another and another until they built an immense pile of gray straight up. And the wind would stop. The birds would grow quiet. Then came something in the air like a thickness, like when my mother stirred flour and water into a soup to give it body. That was what she called it, "body." A soup without body, she claimed, was water with vegetables in it. The air would grow body like my mother's soup, a big gray thickening in the west. And the birds would not only go quiet but were suddenly nowhere to be seen. Where did they go? I bet Jake knew their secret hiding places.

So one of these storms was cooking on the horizon by the time I got home, the first part, anyway, when the dark clouds build on each other. Eugenie knew these storms too, of course, but only from the castle where the reaction was shuttering windows and caring for nervous horses. Her first storm on the farm, she told me, had been with ripe wheat when every walking-and-talking soul went into the field to save as much wheat as possible before the flattening winds swept in like dragon breath. Children and old people, too. Even some who couldn't walk well or couldn't cut and haul, sharpened blades and brought water to the thirsty.

Eugenie did love her dragons when she was telling me stories. Never a real one but all the kinds of dragons that were useful in telling about wild or dangerous things. She'd once described Arbuckle and Jake as particular kinds of dragons.

I wasn't so quick to use dragons, but this storm as the light faded, did have the sun behind it, and instead of all gray, it glowed at the edges orange with yellow brightness along the clouds. If I was going to bring in dragons, this would have been the storm to do it. It was like fire and water had come together in the final hour of the day and had then added lightning to make the whole brilliant sky-soup glow and rumble.

There was nothing we could do. My father rushed us to the barn to feed the animals something extra special to take their minds off the lightning and thunder. Then we bolted the barn door, locked the window shutters, gathered tools and waited. My father and mother claimed these rare storms cleared not only the air but also the minds of people. I couldn't see how and never would, but I had learned to keep my doubt to myself. And anyway, my parents always said this about clearing the air and minds, not like it was something they could actually prove, but more like something they had grown used to repeating and repeating because it made them feel better. Or safer. Or just to say it because they always had said it. I understood that and went along with it. I also learned that there were some old things that I'd say too without even thinking about them. "Long thread, lazy girl." That had been my favorite. I'd say that without even knowing what it was about. Then I finally figured out it meant that if you were sewing some tear or patching something, it would hold better if you used a couple short threads because each one held together separately and the patch wouldn't fall off if one thread broke.

The storm came dragons and all, and I thought of Eugenie in the castle. But more important, I thought of all the wedding preparations sitting out on the summer lawns waiting to be assembled. And I thought of the flower gardens for miles around waiting for what Eugenie called the "looting," armies of servants with baskets to pick every last blossom for the state event that Arbuckle's wedding had become. Not only would the wheat be flattened, but every flower with a long stem would join the wheat stalks splatted like wet hair after a bath.

When the rain finally came, it came with wind that jabbered through the trees and around the barn corners like a hundred voices talking at once. In our farmhouse, we could hear the voices, but we just couldn't make out what they were saying.

In the castle, the voices would have so many corners to blow around that voices would turn to whistles and stomping feet and moaning. The slate roof would clatter. The gargoyles would sputter as rain ran off the tiles and shot out their mouths. I could picture Eugenie already longing for her garden. If she had been on the farm she would be out staking up flowers in the wild wind. But there in the castle, certainly she would sit thinking her gardener's thoughts and looking out her window at the wall of rain.

Before long we sat together again on our appointed garden bench. But wait. First you have to know that the old man and old woman's garden, alone in the whole region, looked exactly the same after the storm as it had before. Not a petal had fallen, not a stem bent. Eugenie smiled when she saw it. I didn't. It made no sense, and, as I said, I had a hard time with things that made no sense. Rain and wind had come to us all, but for some reason, or lack of reason, I think, had not fallen on this particular place as if some invisible dome had protected it. I know. I know. The way to explain it was magic. Magic old woman, witch or double witch! But I didn't know what to think, but Eugenie didn't want to talk about why. She just kept saying over and over that IT was going to happen and we had to be ready. IT indeed. What?

"We might have to stand side by side and speak as one person," Eugenie said. "The castle is completely crazy.

They all think the wedding is going to bring everything together at once: the old ways, history of our people, the passing of the old ones and the rise of the new ones, some big change that will unite all of us under one banner and..." she paused and blew out through her pursed lips, "...and lots and lots of stuff I have no idea about. Some kind of joining and converging and something someone called 'all the new and old gods combining to bless the State at the moment of Arbuckle's wedding.' Lots of hoping fors and expectings. And there was lots more stuff said by the old people at the castle that sounded to me after a time like boiling water or the noises the cows make when lots of gas comes out their back ends. Especially June." And she laughed.

But I couldn't laugh with her, sitting in the shining garden that had enchanted its way out of the storm. The old man and old woman nowhere in sight but maybe everywhere. The great nodding heads of dahlias that didn't grow old, of stalky delphiniums that didn't need to be staked up. I felt like Arbuckle must have felt when everything had seemed out of whack (two girls, one face) but he hadn't been able to say exactly what that was.

Chapter Five

The farm was running itself. Eugenie's flower garden, like all the gardens in the area except one, was flattened by the storm. Representatives from the castle came around looking at the damage, writing things down, shaking their heads. They asked, politely I should add, if we could fix as much as possible, save what we could for the wedding. My father grunted his approval. "We'll try," was somewhere in the grunt. I decided that after my chores I would go to the castle, work a little disguise magic of my own and see if I could get in and help Eugenie. She must have a mess on her hands, I thought.

So early afternoon I set out. I had used the fine clay from down at the creek to color my hair a lighter brown. I had dressed up in what I liked to think of as a sort of joke on the local customary dress that included tassels on my boots, small jingly bells around the cuffs of my blouse and a wide black belt. No one actually wore these all together but each one was somewhere in our little fashion landscape. The total effect, I thought, was something that the castle people might imagine if left on their own. I knew that the castle men and women paid very little attention to what the people working the farms wore. It was that old ladder: I'm up here; you're down there. A pretty tiresome ladder since everything they ate and had — and *were* — came from the land, and we were the ones making the land give its bounty.

In the castle, I always had to be careful bringing up this subject, but there was one place I could. I had a tutor who had learned very quickly that I wanted to be able to talk about and discuss things rather than just be told things. I had let him know early on that his job would last a lot longer if we could talk about ideas. And I included the sun and the moon and (for Eugenie) dirt and water. And, of course, how countries came to think about themselves, and how they told stories to help them remember who they were. And this way I brought up how the King and the Queen and each royal blood walking the hallways of the castle came from the land. That was one idea. And then I brought up lots of ideas that made him very uncomfortable. I had to admit I enjoyed it when he squirmed as I wondered aloud about the difference between my royal family's blood and the stable boy's: Could we see the difference? If we looked very closely? Better blood and worse blood? Was there better stuff in one than the other?

I walked along my very familiar path toward the castle. Eugenie and I had nearly worn it out over time swapping places, switching lives. Very soon I jingled my way to the castle walls. I knew many ways in that did not involve guards. And also I knew that with the wedding coming, so many new people bustled about the castle that no one would bother about an extra girl with tassels on her boots. I used the garden door that Eugenie had recommended a long time ago, the door she had used to sneak out to work with the gardener when she was little.

The door was small and wooden and made so you had to duck to get through without hitting your head. Eugenie thought they had made it that way as a kind of safety feature. No attacking soldiers could get through easily. The gardener would get used to it. But they didn't suspect how much of a door to delight it had become for Eugenie. She told me that even the crack at the bottom, the way the light glittered there, made her feel shivery delicious all over. Because every day she was allowed to play in the garden was like some kind of special tasty dessert to her. So the door, the light, the pegs to hang her dirty clothes, these had all become part of the dessert feeling too.

I waited to make sure no stray gardener or workman was near the door and crept in. Immediately the smell of the castle surrounded me. And I started to wonder first, what Eugenie would think of me showing up, and second, what I could do in a short time.

The door creaked. Voices outside, the banging of tools. I eased down the hall and the head gardener came in out of the bright light. I knew he wouldn't be able to see very much until his eyes got used to the dark. I scurried deeper into the castle and waited in the shadow of a lower hallway. Whomever I met would be the first test of my disguise. I kept my head down. My bells jingled. Not much of a chance to really sneak anywhere with my bells on. There was bundle of painted sticks—I had no idea what they were for—so I picked them up. Now I had an excuse to be wandering the halls. I would say I was taking the sticks to the...to the wedding garden. They were for the... I wouldn't really have to explain what they were for, I guessed. I'd just say some one told me to take them to the garden and leave them there after they were finished. That should do it. Unfinished painted sticks. Nice ones, too. Taking them somewhere for someone. I was all set to go.

I couldn't be sure where Eugenie was, but I knew some obvious places to look. With each set of stairs and new hallway, I climbed out of the lower castle into the royal section. Still, no one tried to stop me. And then.

"Where are you going with those sticks?" asked an ancient maid. I knew her well. This was going to be a test.

I kept my head down at first, trying to help my disguise. But I quickly realized the old woman fell for the clothes immediately. I was, for her, clearly from the country and needed her direction.

"I was told to bring these up the main hall and then

wait. Someone is supposed to come and tell me what to do with them." I set down the stick bundle and leaned it against the stone wall.

With each stairway going up, the castle smelled better and better. I had begun the practice of perfuming the walls below so the sweet lavender rose up the stairs and lightly scented the halls and wall hangings. Eugenie had sniffed when I mentioned it. She confessed to liking the slightly bitter smell of the castle as you went lower until near the door the walls smelled like nasturtiums—nose twisters, flowers that stink. I thought she liked it because when the smell was the strongest, she was about to go out into her beloved garden.

I waited while the maid decided what to do with me. I trusted that all the unusual traffic of the past months had opened my way to go anywhere. The maid harrumphed, and even snorted a little, while she thought. Finally, she allowed that I should do as I was told and take my sticks wherever it was I supposed to go.

"Yes, madam." I made the country-mistake on purpose. Maids weren't called madam. She rolled her eyes as she thought she ought to. And I confess I loved playing the part of myself, the farm girl, though I knew very well all the right castle moves too. Something about being one thing inside the other and fooling around with the world. Well, it just made me want to giggle.

I picked up my sticks and carried them to the next gatekeeper. This younger maid I knew very well, so I changed my voice the best I could. Again, I put the sticks down, leaning them against wall, and made my case that someone told me to take them somewhere. And I was set free again. I almost *did* giggle that time.

I worked my way to where I thought Eugenie was. This was the first time both of us had been in the castle at the same time. And there was only a certain amount of disguise possible if we somehow got caught standing side by side. On the farm all this was easier. Maybe because the barn and Jake and the fields were the perfect scene for the disguise to work. But here, I crept along carrying my silly sticks as a disguise. I supposed I could hold them up and peer through them as if I were looking out of a grove of very skinny trees. Again my inclination to giggle tickled up my nose, but I kept it down. The next hallway was dark but familiar.

Here was where I had carried out my mouse experiments. Live mouse, dead mouse, all in the name of teaching the kingdom how bad the water had become. I smiled to myself remembering the smell of the sick castle, the dull eyes and groaning.

My sticks had now become a clumsy burden, but I couldn't get rid of them just yet. I might need them one final time. And, just then, Corrine came around the corner, and up went my sticks. She had known Eugenie all her life—nanny, social coordinator, and often substitute mother. Corrine stopped dead in her tracks.

"You there. Where are you going with those? They belong in the garden."

I made my voice as scratchy and low as possible, like I was afraid to talk. "I was just—just looking for someone to approve...that is, to say if these were okay. Someone told me to get approval from the castle...people...the, I think, people who...approve these. The colors." I held the sticks up for inspection in the dark hallway, and Corrine insisted I bring them into the light. And then it happened. For a long, long moment she stared at me through the poles as if trying to make out the person on the other side. Was she looking at the poles or me? I could hardly breathe. Maybe this was it, the time when everything collapsed.

But, you know what? She was looking at the poles! She was inspecting the paint on the poles, carefully going over the order of the colors. Colors and the order of colors were very important, I had learned. I hadn't thought of it until just then: castle colors on top, then in order of ancient names each color descended from there down to the lowest pale green of a small, new part of the kingdom in the west. Corrine was running down the color code in her head, moving her lips as she seemed to read the order. The magic word I had said was, "colors."

"Fine. Fine," she said, finally. "Those are correct. Take them to whoever sent you. I would like to clear up these, and these. Make those separations clearer. Do those over. The rest are fine." And she babbled on about duty and correctness and the power of tradition. I began to breathe again, peeking through the sticks, trying to keep the sticks in the light and me out of it. "Go, go. And be quick." She waved me away like sweeping a cobweb from a windowsill.

I had got past her to find Eugenie. But now I had to go back the way I came toward darker and danker. Looking for a new way, I wondered if there was another disguise I could use, so I could get rid of the sticks. And then it came to me—the kitchen.

I had spent enough time in the kitchen to bother the Queen. She said she didn't want me consorting there. That's how she put it: "consorting." As if I would lose my whole princess business by hanging around with lesser creatures. But what I had been there for in the first place was for all the wonderful secrets those "creatures" knew. They knew not only the sauce secrets but the vegetable-into-flowers secrets and the way to make meats perfect and juicy. So many secrets, that was why I'd hung out there.

I worked my way out the tiny door, left the sticks near the wedding preparations, came back in and headed to the kitchen. This could be tricky. The kitchen people knew me as well as anyone. They'd see right through the disguise. And then it hit me. I'd be Eugenie again and get some food and take it up to the other Eugenie. Clothes. I needed clothes, and I had no way to get at those clothes up in the princess rooms. So I decided to try out the gardening clothes hanging by the tiny door.

While being princess I had to pretend, at first, to want to garden as much as Eugenie had. But after doing just enough to make it seem I was Eugenie, I'd stopped. There were so many more interesting things to do. And I had got my tutors trained to give me better and longer lessons in the things that interested me. The numbers, the writing, the measuring—all my favorites.

The clothes hanging by the door still had mud on the knees. The big boots there fit perfectly, of course. The vest with all the pockets for tools, the straw hat, the waxed coat for rain—I dressed quickly and stopped to check myself. This would be a fine disguise. I was myself disguised as myself pretending to be Eugenie. This time I couldn't stop the giggle. It all seemed so silly, in some ways. Here we were again, two girls trying to save the kingdom from itself, from its own wrong headedness. I drew myself up tall, put on the hat and set out.

The kitchen folk barely noticed me as I walked in. They had become so used to me poking about and asking questions, they knew that getting out food was more important than being polite to the princess, so they worked on. There were so many people in the castle now, so much food to get out many times a day, that the kitchen buzzed like a hive of bees. I found an old friend, Jess Andrews, who gave me a quick smile that meant "no time to talk today." And she was off. I found a tray, scrounged some food and sneaked out the back door.

Carrying food anywhere in the castle these days was perfectly normal. Everyone was in a tizzy and, as I think you know, tizzies make people hungry. So off I stalked through the halls now half Alyssa, half Eugenie, my disguise splitting the difference. I could have been carrying food for myself or for someone else. Before this wedding business, a princess, never mind one dressed in homespun with mud on her knees, would never carry her own food. But the rules all went out the window. The gathering of dignitaries and the chatter that would follow was of such enormous importance that the wedding had really become less central than the political deals, the children matched up for future weddings and the old friendships renewed.

And, as sometimes happens, what could go wrong did. Arbuckle Beauregard the Third came down the hallway with the light behind him. He was the minister of water, the savior of the kingdom (with a little help from Eugenie and me) and the bridegroom to be.

Because the light was bright behind him, all I could see was his walk. But he could see me perfectly well and stopped me. He paused. Studied me. I offered him some food to distract him, but he only peered harder at me.

I could see he was taking into consideration the clothes, my hair—everything. Like a big old crow, he turned his head first one way and then another. I felt like a worm he was deciding to eat, or not. Finally, he took a deep breath and said, "Welcome back, Alyssa."

So he knew we had switched back for a while and that now I was here again, dressed in Eugenie's gardening clothes and pretending to be her. Of course, since he knew the whole switch business and had for a long time, and he had benefitted from it more than anyone, I thought he might just let it all go. But he seemed to want me to know that he knew it was me and was on to whatever the two of us were planning. He harrumphed. He turned me again into the light and gave me the bird business. Then he smiled. "Whatever you two are doing, I hope you will not be up to any funny business during my wedding. It's the event of the season, you know. You know! Of course, how could you not know?"

I stuttered a little to get going and then, "Well, Arbuckle. My congratulations to you from both the countryside and the castle." I thought he might appreciate the cleverness of my double congratulations in keeping with my double life. He did.

"Alyssa"—and here he looked over his shoulder like a conspirator checking for who might overhear—"you and Eugenie have been well appreciated by my illustrious family, I can assure you. Your secret is safe with me. But, again, I would like you to not create any problem for my wedding. It's important. It's, well, key to the whole…the entire…."

And then he couldn't seem to find what exactly it was important to, so he finally settled on "everything." It hung in the air, everything, as if the world might stop turning, the summer not arrive without his wedding. It seemed to satisfy him, too, and he made a sweep with his hand to include, I suppose, everything.

I shifted the tray to the other hand to show that it was heavy and I had to be on my way. He gestured me down the hallway, straightened the green vest he always wore now as water-master, and scurried on his way. I passed his test, whatever it was.

Suddenly it occurred to me where Eugenie would be. Not in her chambers, and certainly not anywhere near the kitchen. She would be in the Council chambers.

I had become interested in the workings of the Council and had worked very hard to be allowed to listen to what they talked about, argued about. The King could stop the discussions at any minute—and often did—but he usually wanted to hear all sides before he proclaimed in his deepest voice what his decision was.

The Council chambers were straight ahead and then through two sets of very large wooden doors carved with figures that told the story of the kingdom. The first set, as I approached, were the darkest and oldest, filled with so many shapes that they seemed like wiggling worms poking out of the dark wood. So many old faces, noses wrinkled up, mouths open shouting silently in battle with ancient enemies. The doors were ajar. No one was tending them.

The next set of doors, across a long room with portrait after portrait of the old ones glaring out severely at whoever passed, that was as far as I could go. I couldn't just show up at Eugenie's side and stop whatever proceedings were going on. Not without consulting her first. But I had to find her before someone accidently saw us both together and raised the alarm. I could just hear it: Imposter! Imposter! Yes, fake girl and real girl. One a princess and one a what? A princess too. This was going to be interesting. Maybe not fun, but interesting.

I crept into an alcove where I could be quiet in the shadows there. I couldn't hear through the door at all. Maybe nothing was happening in there. How could I get closer?

I liked to think of the castle now as my castle. When we had first switched, I'd made it my business to explore every nook and cranny, every passage way and crawl space. And I'd discovered that sometime in the past they had built passageways in the walls of all the important rooms so that the heat of the kitchen stoves could be directed up inside the wall, not to heat the giant rooms, but to warm the food that was often delivered to the rooms and then kept for a while in the cupboards built into the walls. And these passageways were very narrow but, I found, just big enough to fit a farm girl or a princess. Jake would have hated it in there. You couldn't see. It was close—the opposite of a tree top. It smelled of hundreds of years of being a castle.

The air intake for the wall space was right near my feet in the alcove. And I could hear voices growing louder coming from outside the first set of doors, coming closer to the Council chamber. Without thinking, I pulled the grate out and crept into the space pulling the grate closed behind me. I crouched at first but quickly found I could stand up—sort of. If I bent over I could shuffle through the wall into the Council chamber. I did and suddenly I could hear the voices clearly. With my back against one wall, my knees just rested against the other. It was warm and today smelled like the kitchen's baking, not at all of stinky castle or dank castle. Except for the darkness so thick I couldn't see my hand, it was kind of pleasant, if you didn't mind tight spaces. Sort of like being wrapped in a blanket that smelled like fresh rolls. The voices came to me through a grate at the back of the cupboard.

One old voice announced, "They are happy to contribute from their gardens. I hear from many sources they feel it's their way of being at the wedding. Think of it as a kind of tax they're willing to pay gladly."

Another voice, higher, but deferring to the first voice: "I should think, of course, they would be glad, but I don't know how much money they will lose if we take the flowers and some of their food for the winter. They sell the flowers, I understand. At markets. Then use that money for...for whatever they need, I suppose."

Clearly Eugenie was not in the room, or she was controlling herself, waiting for her chance. I couldn't see anything, just hear.

"On the other hand," a higher voice chimed in. "All the people in the country deserve a chance to contribute to the wedding that will be bringing together important families, securing our—*their!*—borders, and bringing peace for them and their children. A few flowers, some crops— these are the least they can give. The only difficult part is making them understand how useful and valuable their contributions will be. The key here is information!" The voice rose and quavered. "If they knew, they would gladly give. And give again." I could imagine the posturing and dramatic finger pointing to the heavens.

The warm walls were becoming more comfortable as I grew used to the tight fit. But for the voices coming in through the grate, I thought I could have taken a nap. My eyes got heavy for a second, but then...

Another voice, this time very familiar. Mine. Well, Eugenie's. She began low and slow, and then like music searching for the right instruments, she grew full and loud and magnificent.

Chapter Six

"Councilors, ladies and gentlemen." She paused. There was a loud murmur as the councilors tried to understand the idea of a young girl speaking to them. A princess, but a young girl. She kept talking and raised her voice a little to speak over the noise. "And gardeners," she continued. "Gardeners will know right away what's wrong with the plan to take the flowers. And the vegetables. A gardener is a person who knows about growing things in dirt. Very simple. Yes, but also very complicated. A gardener is the one who says 'yes' to all the work and the thinking and the care that makes things grow. Your food and flowers, your life, is possible because there is someone gardening and farming—bigger gardens, really. When a gardener sees a plant is wilting or not growing well, the gardener has to ask why. Water? Sun? Pests? A gardener asks a plant what it needs and then listens. A gardener speaks plant. Are there any gardeners here?"

The silence seemed to go on for a very long time. Some throats cleared and harrumphed. There were no gardeners. "But all of you eat and have flowers for your occasions. All the speakers here today seem to know some things that all the gardeners would do. What those gardeners would like to do with their flowers and vegetables. How would you know that? Did you ask the gardeners?"

"Young lady. Princess Eugenie. These proceedings are for...." This from a voice ancient and scratchy, one not used to being told about the world by a young person. I almost laughed as I thought, this would be the perfect time for me to come jumping out of the wall and echoing Eugenie, waving my muddy knees around the room. Maybe hooting a little like an owl. All this occurred to me as Eugenie was interrupted and the Council murmured over the scolding that they were sure was to come. But, of course, I didn't really jump out of the wall, though it would have been very interesting. This was Eugenie's time. I knew what she would think of the old man's interruption. She spoke sharply without raising her voice.

"You are interrupting. You may speak when I finish." The murmur added a few gasps. "Then you may have your opinion. And I might ask if you are a gardener. But I think I already know the answer. I believe what you are doing is suggesting that your ignorance is more important than my knowledge of gardening and gardeners."

The stunning silence, then the clatter and cacophony that followed seemed to feed on the word strange to these halls, "gardeners." Oh, my warm walls felt delicious, I can tell you. Eugenie was out in the cold, all right. Maybe I would have to pop out of the wall after all. I was sure it was the word "ignorance" that rattled the Council walls. An old Councilor ignorant? I could hear words and parts of words: "The nerve...insolent...princess or not...who does she think she is...young...her father...." And the buzz rose.

I strained at the grate to see anything, something, except the ceiling. I was sure Eugenie had her hands on her hips, though. I had seen her defiant stance before and had marveled at it. Something very princess in it; something very farm-girl gardener. Her birth position and the smell of freshly turned dirt joined together into an astounding girl. And astounding she was. I waited.

The next clear voice was another scratchy old one. But this one said, "Let her talk. She's right about too many people who know nothing saying too much." And then silence again. Then Eugenie.

"Thank you. I will try to help you understand what

a farmer and gardener feel for what they bring from the ground. It is a beet or a flower, yes. But it is also the thing that we start from a seed and care for as a shoot and then fuss over as a young plant. We watch it bud out, stretch for the sun, stretch roots for dirt and become what we saw in the seed. Even a field of grain has a first green haze when the small plants are fragile and tender. Then they explode into a grain field and promise to feed us. Gardeners can't walk past their plants without checking on them. The listening to plants again. The learning to speak plant. And you ask if a gardener will miss the flowers and vegetables, will stand by as workers come and loot their gardens? They *will* let you loot only because you have the army. Because you have the cannons. The time has come to ask them if they will sell, *sell,* their care and hard work for the wedding." More murmuring here, loud enough that I couldn't hear Eugenie for a short time. I thought the talking was either agreement with her or, maybe, complete disagreement. I couldn't tell which. Maybe she was being escorted out of the room. But no. I could hear her again.

"So, Councilors and planners, King, Queen and those who will be wed, I ask you to think like a gardener even if you're not one. Not only for the wedding plans, but every day that food is wasted or allowed to spoil. When flowers go unwatered. When you pass fields and gardens someone has made and tended. If you can think like a gardener, then you can think like a soldier who is afraid to die or a hungry person who needs food. Begin thinking like a gardener and the kingdom will become a better place every day and in many ways. Thank you."

I took a deep breath in the silence that filled the chamber. Then one person clapped, then another. And then, maybe someone important began clapping because the applause scattered in the room like a flock of birds. I imagine it was the King clapping for his daughter that let the others join in. I would ask Eugenie later. But it was clear even from my hiding place that not everyone in the room was clapping. I imagined hard stares, pursed lips, glances away.

Whatever Council business remained to be discussed was dropped. Eugenie's speech hung in the air like unfinished business. The room still echoed: ignorance, gardens, think like a gardener. And, I should mention, heat. Suddenly my cramped quarters in the wall got very warm. Maybe it was the heat from the kitchen rising, but maybe it was the heat from the room where all the councilors ears must have turned red with Eugenie's words. I still couldn't see what was going on. I couldn't leave the wall until everyone filed out of the chamber. I could—and did—scrunch down and wait.

When I couldn't hear any voices or footsteps, I waited even longer to be sure I was alone. Then I tried to leave the wall the way I got in. The grate was stuck. I must have pulled it hard when I went in. I tried kicking it on the top so it would open without scratching the floor and leaving a trace of my entry. Somehow it had swelled up, maybe from the heat. I worked back toward the cupboard in the Council chamber, and wiggled myself up to the space on the shelf that was supposed to warm the plates of food. And then like a snake crawling out of its hole in a rock wall, I scrunched myself up then stretched out and inched my way out the slot at the back of the dark cupboard. Now I was lying along a top shelf. What a fine surprise I would make if someone opened the cupboard door looking for plates and found me instead.

I couldn't help it. It was funny to imagine. I giggled.

"Who's there," came a voice from the room.

I froze. No place to go. If someone opened the door...

But no one opened the door. I could barely hear the swish of a broom finishing the job of cleaning up. I lay on the shelf feeling like some kind of stockpile of nosey girl. I waited until well after the sweeping stopped. Then I pushed open the cupboard door very slowly and peeked out. I was alone. Now to get off this top shelf and not crash to the floor. I slid out, slithered down, slunk away into a shadow. In the next room I could hear the broom again, so I waited. And waited.

Finally, the next room had no sounds. The light was growing dim in the windows. Evening had come. I had spent my chance to plan with Eugenie waiting in a wall, lying on a shelf. One last try, then I had to rush back to the farm.

I skulked from room to room ready with fresh alibis about suddenly wearing my gardening clothes but didn't need them. I went as directly as I could to Eugenie's chambers. Empty. I even thought about hiding under her bed and then popping out after she retired for the night. But then I'd be missed at home, and they might send people out looking for me. I thought that somewhere in the castle Eugenie was either being celebrated for her speech or, just as likely, she was seated with her head down listening to a lecture from her father. Or mother. I couldn't wait to find out which, but for now, I had to slink out of the castle and get home before the light was completely gone.

Back ways, dark halls, once waiting until a worker passed, then out the small garden door, Eugenie's garden clothes back on their pegs. The castle lights glowed behind me. And soon I saw another glow.

The old couple's garden, ahead of me and down the path, seemed lit up from the inside in some way. The flowers were not only fresh looking, but they seemed to have some kind of light shining on them. It might have been a trick of the evening light. It might have been my tired eyes, my weary soul, my side aching from being a cupboard dweller, but these flowers were not just growing in this early summer light, they were efflorescing. I think I have that word right. Almost like they had taken up all the color they could and now were capturing bright colors from butterflies and flashes of hues from birds. I sat down to rest and watched. Not a person stirred in house or garden. Small smoke trailed up out of the chimney.

Everything around seemed to be waiting with me. I found myself holding my breath in the still and thickening air. I wasn't sure exactly what I was waiting for, but I couldn't leave. As noisy as the Council chamber had been, this garden was the same intensity but quiet. I don't know how long I sat waiting, but the light held and held until it seemed the world had stopped to wait too. And then, after a short time that was hard to tell how long, a small breeze came up and seemed to set everything in motion again.

I took the path around the garden, and even when it was at my back, I could feel the glow there as if plants could smile.

I made it into the barn just as my mother was calling me from the house. I tossed a little hay on myself, brushed most of it off, and made my way to the house. And then I noticed Jake high in a maple tree seeming to sway at the thin end of branch like some ripe fruit. The breeze continued to pick up, and he rode there as if he might just fly off into the sky.

Altogether a very strange afternoon. I have to admit that I prefer my afternoons simple and focused and reasonable—farm or castle, either place. Flirting with the spiders in the castle walls, being gobsmacked by a glowing garden, Jake ascending to the heavens—too much for a tired girl. I wondered how Eugenie was feeling.

The next morning I asked my mother to tell me what she knew about the old couple and their garden.

"Not much, really," she said. "That is, I don't *know* much of anything. But I've heard many things. You always hear things about people who keep mostly to themselves. But, dear, what you know and what you hear about people should always be kept separate in your head."

She paused and looked at me to make sure I knew the difference. I nodded and made sure she knew I was paying attention. She was a good storyteller, but she always tried to include some kind of lesson about living a good life. Sometimes that lesson ran over the story a little. You had to wait for the lesson and then she would continue.

"People say they lost a child. And that's a very difficult thing for anyone. But they say that the old couple took it very hard. No one saw them at all for almost two years. And then they would show up at the market on Saturdays to sell flowers and vegetables. And their flowers, especially, were the best anyone had ever seen. They lasted longer and were bigger and brighter than any other flowers. Some people—and you would know these people if I told you their names; they still talk like this today—well, these people immediately thought there was some kind of witchcraft involved. That both of them, man and woman, had become witches and used evil powers to make such flowers as the ones they sold in the market place. And these people were quick to make something evil out of a thing as beautiful as well-tended flowers. They still do. Whatever is beyond them, they think must be wrong and somehow evil." She paused and rolled her eyes for effect. "The plain term for this kind of thinking is: stupid. They are stupid people. And there will always be stupid people in life."

I knew the lesson was coming and waited.

She looked at me, and I nodded though I didn't know exactly what I was nodding about. Then she continued.

"How you deal with stupid people will be a test of your character all life long. I prefer the smile-and-leave technique. It works best for me. But each person must find their own way in this matter. Your father...well, your father has a different way. *Had* a different way, I should say. When he was younger he would snap back at the stupid part, not let a word go by without stuffing it back into the stupid mouth it came out of. Since he is a big man, this also had the effect of stopping the stupidity for a while. Same as my way. But my way had the advantage of not making enemies. So you may choose. Find your own way."

As important as this was, the story of the old couple seemed to be getting lost in the lesson about how to deal with stupidity. I would wait. She always came back to the story.

"So those people who said they were witches, *must be* witches if they could grow those unnatural flowers, well, they were always looking for other people who believed the same way. And if they found enough of them, they would help each other to more and more unpleasant conclusions. After a short time, and enough other stupid people nodding in agreement, the old couple was said to eat children, walk with the evil spirits at night, chant songs in a language nobody else knew, boil big pots of strange animals and animal parts, and turn animals into people and people into animals. I think that's most of what they began to believe. There might have been even more. It's funny how that list was the usual things people say against something they don't understand."

My mother rolled her eyes again, and I steadied myself for the next lesson on how to live. But I think she realized that I didn't need it spelled out. I'd got the idea.

"And then one day, enough of those—what should we call them?—those 'easily swayed people,' gathered at a farm near here and marched over to the old couple's house. I believe they were going to confront them. Or drive them away. Or maybe burn them. I don't know. We'll never know, because the whole group came back from their march shaking their heads. Not one of them could remember what had happened. And even more important, not one of them could remember what they had gone there to do. We, your father and I, found them all wandering in our field, all fifteen or twenty of them, looking as if they had had too much beer to drink. Or as if they had become completely lost and had not yet found their way. Of course, we knew most of them from the market days, but they could only agree that they had gone some place together and now could not remember what for."

She turned to look out the window in the direction of the old couple's farm. She sighed.

"It's very hard to lose a child, I think. Their flowers became their children. Something to care for and…"

My mother stared out the window as if she too had lost a child. But as far as I knew she hadn't. Or she didn't tell me if she had. Maybe she just understood somehow.

I asked, "Has anyone tried to talk to them?"

"We all tried, at some time or another. We took food and tried to talk. But it was so long ago, and most of us were so much younger than they were, and we, well, we just didn't understand enough. And so we tried to talk to them and be neighborly. They were polite. Asked us to sit down. Brought water to drink. But somehow they let us know they were better off being by themselves. And so little by little we left them completely alone. We thought they would come find us if they needed help. Or someone to talk to. We offered. And finally, they seemed more real in the stories we told about them than they were in life. They were over there, and we were over here."

I thought about Jake. He went wherever he wanted, on the ground or in the trees. I wondered if he had seen the old couple or talked to them. Jake talked to anybody—any time. He could have wandered over to their house and jabbered his jabber at them if he felt like it. I didn't think Jake would recognize anything in the world stranger than himself; it was his powerful way of going through life.

Mother clapped her hands together, maybe to signal the end of our conversation, maybe to swat an insect I couldn't see. "Anyway, that's why we let them be. Their flowers are a kind of symbol of both their sadness and their way of dealing with the sadness."

Chapter Seven

Eugenie and I were each in the place we were born to, each longing to return to the other one's place we had come to love—that was our situation for days. Days dragged on like this. I couldn't wait to find out how her time in the castle had been affected by her speech to the Council.

I sent her a message to make a meeting date. No answer. I sent again. No answer. She had disappeared into the castle. I had to find out what happened. I pictured her in the dungeon. Then I pictured her locked in her rooms. That was more likely. They wouldn't throw a princess, their own daughter, into a nasty dungeon, I don't think. I had to go to the castle—again—and find out.

The wedding preparations were now making a spectacular mess for almost a mile around the castle. There were wagons piled high with colorful flags or banners waiting to be put in place. The roads were being rebuilt with cobblestones and fresh gravel so the approach to the castle seemed to have glowing, new stones like glittering arrows to show where the celebration would be. There were camps of workers strewn across the hillside and muddy paths leading down to the work sites. Then the food preparers had set up in lower spots to feed the workers. Closer to the castle it seemed an entire carpenter shop was established with young men on treadmills walking fast to drive belts attached to pulleys that had more belts driving machines that made spindles and spires and every sort of shaped wood. I could smell the fresh pine and cedar being made into what I supposed were important chairs and benches for important men and women's bottoms. Of course, there would be cushions of red with yellow trim and deep blues with light green trim—the Queen's favorites. And then each visiting state would sit on a bench with their own colors. The pillow makers were hard at work in rows beneath awnings that shaded them from sun or kept off rain as they worked. A whole village, two villages, had sprung up along the road. There was a general tizzy with quick-stepping and urgent shouts.

I paused on the road to admire the scene. Eugenie would find this whole business completely disgusting; I know she would. She would say it was wasteful, silly and pretentious.

The pretend part, the being something you weren't, the false and empty faking, the special kind of lie that all this represented—that was what would anger her.

Me? I was of two minds. First of all, this whole spectacular kind of circus was just plain interesting to look at. New people, new colors, music and play and work that you hadn't seen before. I found that very pleasing. And second, I understood (and so did Eugenie, to be truthful) that spending all that money on a wedding, and the wedding of a known goofball on top of it, was really an investment in a kind of social plan, a compact. That was the word the Queen used—compact. A deal. An agreement. And all of the compact had future reasons for the present extravagance. The kingdom was planting seeds, sort of, for a future crop of marriages and agreements and everyone's safety. That was what the thinking was. One time, I overheard the King and councilors pondering the advantages of the great wedding expense. It all seemed to me to be counting chickens before they were hatched—future chickens, very expensive chickens that could never lay enough eggs to get back their original cost. But I was just a visiting princess. What did I know?

There was a great noise at the castle gate and everyone

looked up and paused. It was Beauregard Arbuckle the Third coming out the main gate to inspect the scene. And immediately I knew that I couldn't let him see me again. I reached down to the muddy roadside and dipped my fingers in the warm goo and rubbed my hands together and then dirtied my face. I tucked my princess hair up into a cap and drew my hands up into my sleeves. What else? I was far enough away that Arbuckle wouldn't see me for a while. But if I was going to get into the castle and discover what had happened to Eugenie, I would have to have business there, business that could include my mud disguise. Oh, what job could a mud-faced young girl have that would require her to go into the castle and wander the halls until she found Eugenie? That was my problem.

I looked around as if somehow I would see something that could solve that problem. There were so many people, young and old, that out there I could float from one group to the next without difficulty. Arbuckle's inspection party came closer and closer. Then I saw my chance.

A cart loaded with beets and turnips had paused in the roadway and the farmer was looking for a way to let the inspection party past. I crept up behind the cart where the farmer couldn't see me and grabbed one bundle of beets and one of parsnips, both with their leaves tied together like a bouquet of flowers. With my arms full and the leaves covering my face I popped out from behind the cart just as the group approached and waited for the farmer to clear the road. The beets and parsnips were still covered in the dirt that would be the logic of my disguise—farm girl with dirty face carrying food to the kitchens, kitchens everywhere in the castle now that feeding the hoards of new people had become a full-time job.

I had my disguise and my reason for being in the halls of the castle. And the farmer was so flustered trying to get out of the way of the royal party, well, the semi-royal party, anyway, that he didn't notice me passing him by and curtsying my way past Arbuckle who never even glanced at me. His nose was pointed vaguely at the sky as if something didn't smell quite right. His green water-master vest had been replaced with a brocade vest in castle colors. He wore a single earing. He snuffed as I passed. Traces of the old Arbuckle.

In his party were a number of people who might have recognized me. But my root vegetables held high, my edible bouquet, magically allowed me to pass and approach the castle. Behind my leaves I snickered and took a bite of the leaf of the smallest beet. I always loved the littlest beet leaves with the deep red vein running up the middle. It was like eating a delicious little map.

Inside the castle no one said a word to me. Girls carrying food were not remarkable here any more. I said yes ma'am and no sir and curtsied and bowed my head in passing. Like a silly dance, I thought. Again. I was getting good at it. In this dance I had complete sympathy with Eugenie and her dislike for empty gestures.

The first person to look at me carefully stopped me just outside Eugenie's chambers.

"Princess Eugenie! How did you get out? Wait. Wait," the maid said excitedly. "You know you can't be out here." And she swept her cloak over me to hide me and began to whisper. "You'll get us all in trouble, Princess. You agreed to stay in your rooms until the King…" She looked around wide-eyed and hid me further in her great cloak. "Let's get you back inside quickly."

I figured out immediately what was going on. But I also thought the less I said the better off I'd be. The better off *we* would be. Maybe all of us, including the maid.

She unlocked the chamber door with a huge key fastened around her waist with a white ribbon. I had never seen the key before, maybe because the rooms had never been locked.

The maid continued whispering to me as she worked the big key. "How did you get out? And where did you get these clothes? And what did you do out here?"

She gave no time for answers between rushed questions. Finally, she cranked the key twice around and something clanged inside the door, and it opened. She pushed me in very quickly and shut the door. I supposed that all the hush and rush would somehow become clear, but there I stood returned to my rooms that now felt as if I had been tossed into a dungeon. It was a very nice dungeon, though.

All the rough walls were hung with story-telling tapestries. The stories began with simple rabbits and other woodland creatures nibbling their way across a green and gold landscape while a farmer stopped to wipe his brow. In the distance was a house with smoke curling out the chimney, in the far distance a mountain or high hill, and in the very far distance the sun was broken into rays and glowing fabric to give the whole tapestry a wonderful sense of depth. Then down the hallways came the more complicated stories. I knew these were history stories about the founding of the kingdom: boars and bears, and even lions, fought fierce battles surrounded by armies of men with lances. I always thought the men with lances looked very bored and tired of the whole business. But row after row of battle figures seemed to be joining reluctantly in some great war that, of course, was frozen in the woven moment forever. I imagine the weavers put some of their own tiredness into the faces of the closest men.

And down the hallway was room after room that I knew well. At the far end was my favorite. It was smaller than the other room, the ceiling was lower and the fireplace smaller. But the room warmed up quickly, there was a very big chair and good light streaming in a high window. It was a fine place to read. It was also the perfect place just to be alone, to sit and be alone with whatever doll I wanted to talk to, whatever daydream I wanted to follow.

And there by the fire sat Eugenie.

I had walked in so quietly that she hadn't heard me until I entered the room. Her surprise quickly turned to delight, then to worry.

"I can't believe you came here," she scolded, after first giving me a great hug. "This is risking everything we have worked for. They'll see us together and then...and then the whole game is done."

"Game?" I said. "Maybe that's the problem. It was all a game until they decide to lock you up for saying the truth. I think the game is over any way you look at it."

"Well, that's exactly what happened, you know," she said. I was going to tell her that I knew about the speech and everything *except* the locking up part, but I decided to wait. She went on, "First they politely applauded my little speech"—(little speech? I thought, is that what she calls telling off the councilors and calling the oldest ones ignorant?)—"then, after everyone had left, my father took me aside and said he had decided, for reasons very complicated and secret, to confine me to my room until the wedding. He said with all the important people coming, he didn't want me running around—that's what he called it, 'running around'—making trouble with all the people who came for the wedding. And for the peacemaking. He really called it 'peacemaking.' He said, with lots of finger wagging and using of the royal 'we,' that it was all about proper order of things, after all was said and done. And that I had made a temporary mess of that order by scolding the Council. Then he sighed and said he would have to work hard to fix what I had broken. But he would do it. For the good of everyone. And he didn't want to discuss it or any sassiness either. And that was that. They tossed me in the dungeon. Well, this dungeon, anyway." She pointed around us at her very pleasant dungeon. "Okay, it's not bad. But it's the principle of the thing. I'm wrong. They're right. Over and done."

She stopped to catch her breath, and I told her I was hiding in the wall and heard the whole thing. The part in the Council room, anyway.

And then she said, "You should have popped out right when I finished and there we would have been, the two of us. Double right! Double spectacular!"

"I thought about it, believe me. And then I thought that if we wanted to get back to places we wanted to be, we'd have to work this out a different way. I look at your garden on the farm and think how much you'd like to be there. And I go through the milking and haying and weeding while longing to get back to my studies in the castle. Some other way. There will have to be some other way."

Eugenie rubbed her hands together like she was getting ready to work on something. I thought she might spit on her palms, but she didn't.

She began slowly and then picked up speed. "Okay, here's what we have to do. The whole castle is fuming at me. Well, *some* are fuming. Some others are just tsking. And tsking some more. And a few are just surprised and maybe waiting for whatever I do next. I don't think I made you any friends, alas."

I could see her sigh was meant in fun, a big fat alas with a little bit of eye roll. But she laughed and went on.

"So where I *did* make you some friends, I think, is in the rest of the kingdom. Apparently no one in the castle had even considered that every garden in the kingdom wasn't the property of the crown. Some kind of ancient right to be alive that all came from God then the King and then from the King's supporters. Everything is the King's because the King was selected by God to be His organizer on earth. I guess I've always known some version of this. We all did. But until that whole idea jumped on everybody's flower garden, I didn't think much of it. It was just an idea. Well, now it's back in the conversation, thanks to me. Thanks to you!"

And there we were again. The whole switching thing had finally come to bite us. What she did was mine to own. What I did was going to be her. If we did nothing, neither of us would have any problems, but doing nothing was suddenly not possible. So she sighed again, and I sighed too.

"Eugenie, do you think we could fix all this by, you know, just telling everybody everything?" I was trying out the idea, something I usually did only in my head. But there it was, hanging in the air.

"That would certainly change everything from the way it is now." She pushed her hair off her forehead in thought. I always thought, "our hair" when she did that.

We stared at each other for a long time. I was thinking what it might be like having everyone know about our wonderful swap: people's big eyes, the whispers behind hands as we walked by together, the whole business of "which one are you?"—that thing twins must get all the time. But even more important than the two of us would be that one of us was illegal. One of us was assaulting a thousand years of the kingdom's bloodlines and privilege. One of us would have to be punished for her cheekiness and her arrogance.

Of course, the other one—Eugenie—would be scolded

and sighed over and lectured on how she risked being injured, how the whole kingdom was counting on her, and she must promise never again to be so silly. I could imagine a giant finger wagging in her sad face while I was hauled off to the dungeon and my parents driven off their farm and Jake was forced into the army at age eight.

I didn't know what Eugenie was thinking, but it wasn't that.

Finally, we both tried to speak at the same time. Stopped. And then did it again. You go first no you go first.

It turns out Eugenie was thinking about my difficult situation but also how awful it would be to spend her life back in what she called the "brittle, empty castle."

"...the brittle, empty castle—that would kill me," she said sadly. "I don't know what I would do." She took a deep breath and let it out slowly. It didn't even qualify as a sigh. It was something else. She seemed to take in all our woes at once and then let them out like blowing out some invisible and unhappy candles. And then after waiting for the air to clear, she said, "You know what we can do?"

Yes, yes, I thought. Hurry up. What can we do? My whole life seemed hanging from a thread that dangled there from Eugenie's thoughts.

"I think we can do anything WE want, what WE think is right. And then make it fit with everything around us. The King, the Queen, our shared mother and father. Jake." She brightened up at her own thought of having everything. "All at once! That's how we spring it. We plop ourselves right in the middle of everything. They won't be able to do a thing about it."

And that's sort of what we did. Here's how we did it. Or how it happened to us, anyway.

Chapter Eight

The plan was simple, but timing was everything. The big wedding was now days away, and the castle was filling with honored guests. I would have to sneak back home the way I got in just so my mother and father wouldn't miss me. Eugenie would have to serve her temporary exile in silence. And I would have to find the old man and the old woman and see if they could help us.

On the way home I passed by the old couple's garden. It was still glowing with bright flowers and around the edges a trellis of beans, lettuce and bursting tomato plants. And, of course, not a dead flower or wilted piece of lettuce. It was as if the whole plot of ground was somehow outside the real world, like a painting on a wall of a beautiful woman who never grew old, never failed to smile like sunshine. I had to hurry home, but there it was. I stopped. Birds hopped through the leaves and branches eating insects as if they had been specially invited to be there. A rabbit sat outside the garden and looked confused by something. All that lettuce, but he didn't hop in and eat any. Finally, he went away, not so much hopping as scooting through the grass back into the woods. This garden would be the first stop for the King's men tomorrow as they came out with wagons to pick fresh flowers for the wedding. I would try to be in a good place to see what happened then. Maybe the rabbit had the right idea. We'd see.

Jake saw me coming before I saw him. Jake saw everything from his perches in the trees. He swung down and landed very near me before I even heard him. Of course, he knew everything about Eugenie and me. But he didn't talk about it. Ever. He called me Alyssa just as if I were the real thing, the real *substitute* thing—that is, Eugenie —he had grown used to. And, as Eugenie had asked me to, I was kind to him, asked about his day, still read to him now and then, and always waved to him when he was high in a tree surveying the farm or whatever he did up there. I wondered aloud if he had seen anything at the old people's place. If he knew anything about them, something only he could see from his perch.

Jake, who was usually a child of many words, only said, "Nope."

"Nope, what?" This was the chore of trying to draw him out. So again I asked. "Nope there's nothing you know or nope there's nothing you can see."

"Just nope." And he walked a little way with me, kind of skipping but more shuffling along the path kicking up dried leaves just to hear them rustle. Then he said in the same tone as the rustling leaves, "They are magic, I think."

Well, there it was. The whole story. I laughed and said that, yes, it was a good guess. There was something going on there that wasn't happening anywhere else, and I guessed that was the definition of magic. Or one definition, anyway. Jake made noises and nodded his head to approve.

"I could find out more," he offered.

And I know I shouldn't have, but I did. He usually seemed to enjoy my silliness. I said, "Unless, they capture you and turn you into a cat or other small animal that would be useful to them. They already have a cat, so it might be…a mouse! To feed the cat! No. That would use up all their magic just for cat food. They might keep you and eat you themselves. Probably have to fatten you up a little." I pinched his arm gently to assess his fatness. He smiled but not his usual smile. Not his "who cares" smile. Clearly he was thinking about being fattened up to be cooked and eaten. I went on; I couldn't help myself. "But at least they will cook you with fresh vegetables. Did you see the tomatoes they have? And the beans. Who else has beans like that?"

He was walking with me but squirming a little too. I used to do this to him when he was little. Mother kept an eye on my fooling and told me not to scare him. Fooling around was fine. But not too far. And as he grew older I had to go further with the fooling to get any kind of reaction from him. So my stories got a little richer, more dangerous, more detailed. Jake said, "Nobody does. Not beans like those."

I knew that Jake was fond of raiding my—Eugenie's—garden for baby beans and tiny carrots with the dirt still on them. Eugenie's plan was to plant enough so he could have all he wanted, especially the small peas with the flower petal still clinging to the pod. He'd pick those by the handful and eat them. So Eugenie's pea row went on and on to both feed the family and the little raider. I asked him, "Did you ever sneak into the old people's garden? Just once?"

He was quiet a long time as we marched along. Then he said, "I was going to. But I didn't." I let him collect his thoughts, and he continued, "I wanted to, that is. I went in the evening, almost dark. But then..." And we walked along in silence again. "Then I got closer and the garden wasn't there. It wasn't where it was. I thought I'd got turned around in the dark so I tried a different way. But it wasn't there again. I sat right down where I thought the middle of the garden had to be. But it was just grass, like the grass at the edge of the woods. That was the only time I did that. It was very, very strange."

Jake was used to saying just what came to his mind. Sometimes the order was not perfect, but I could see the word wheels spinning there behind his eyes, words flitting to and fro anxious to come out.

"Do you think you just got lost in the dark?"

His answer was efficient and full of things left unsaid. "No."

We walked together in that noisy quietness of the woods: leaves under foot, far off birds and close up birds saying bird things to each other. I began to think how lucky Eugenie and I had been to sit on the garden bench among those magic flowers, to sit and talk and catch sight of the old woman and her ghostly watering can filling up the air with invisible water. They must have chosen us to be allowed into the garden. And I began to think back to what I'd really seen there. Eugenie and I had been so intent on our plans and our jabber about everything from the castle and everything from the farm that I hadn't really noticed what was around us. Nice flowers. Clean bench. Something peaceful and welcoming. But what was there? I couldn't say. I didn't remember anything except two girls saving the kingdom. At least that's what I thought at the time.

Jake and I came into the farmyard past the garden. I reached in and got him one of the small peas he loved and tossed it to him. He popped it into his mouth and smiled.

My mother had been looking everywhere for me. She had jobs for me to do. But I was back in enough time, and in the company of Jake, so that she didn't think twice about my absence. Tomorrow would be when all the pieces of this wedding business would come together. Tomorrow would be a very busy day.

The day dawned like one of those early summer surprises, you know, that you weren't expecting until later in the heat of late July. Cicadas sang until it sounded like every tree had a tiny saw screeching away in competition with all the other tiny saws. Birds were about their business with special joy. Maybe they were eating the cicadas. Maybe today the whole thing that Eugenie and I made over these many, many months, maybe that would end today. I planted my feet next to my bed before getting up. I could hear my mother stirring below in the kitchen. It was early but already the day seemed completely on fire.

The King's men and the flower collectors—flower *thieves*, Eugenie would say—arrived in our barnyard and wordlessly set about harvesting every flower in Eugenie's garden. They took the dahlias, the daisies, the baby's breath and the delphiniums—whatever was not damaged by the storm. Big flower or little flower didn't seem to matter; they even took the buds. Silently they worked their way through the garden handing cut flowers to the waiting servants. Behind them the bare-stalk stubble poked up from the brown earth like sorry sticks pointing nowhere.

In a very short time they were done. One of the King's men, one who looked like he was in charge, cornered my father and began to ask him questions in a loud voice so that from across the yard I could hear the questions but not my father's answers.

"Your neighbor, the old people with the garden. I hear they are peculiar. What do you know about them?" he asked.

My father seemed reluctant to say anything. He looked down at his shoes and said something quietly, something very short.

The captain boomed again. "You must know more than that. They have lived right there at the edge of your farm for many years. I have to know more about who they are. Who are they?"

Again, there was a long pause and then my father said a

little something, but I could see it wasn't what the captain wanted to hear, and he spoke up again.

"You know there are other ways to get them to cooperate with us. By law, all land is the King's land. I think you know that. I think they know that. If a whale washes up on the beach, why that whale belongs to the King as sure as he owns the deer in the forest. Your flowers, the old couple's flowers, why even the flowers of the deepest woods—they all belong to the King. I don't see why this is so difficult. My men have been to the old folk's garden, but every time they try to pick the flowers, something happens. We don't know what. But you do. Or someone around here does. And they better speak up soon because our patience is growing very short. If there is magic or foul play, we have to know about it. Where are the old people? Who is hiding them? We have ways of dealing with magic the same as we have soldiers to fight battles."

I could see that my father said nothing, even when the captain paused to take a breath. The captain seemed to be waiting for my father to confess or tell on the old couple. Something! But my father stood with his head bowed listening respectfully. He knew what the soldiers could do to him—to us. He also knew that listening was the least trouble-making thing he could do. I waited. It seemed to me the whole world paused.

The captain continued in his loud voice. "I don't suppose you know anything more than everyone else we've stopped and asked." He suddenly sighed. "This is not going to be easy to explain to the King or to the wedding people. You can see, can't you, this will be bad for me and my family. I have six children." A small whine had crept into his voice. "We are all asking you to tell me something to take to the King so that I don't lose my job. My head!"

My father quietly said something that I couldn't hear.

The captain put his hand on my father's shoulder but not in a mean way. It looked to me as if he were asking for sympathy from my father more than threatening him. I wanted to edge closer to be able to hear better, but as soon as I tried and my father saw me and shooed me away with the back of his hand. I stayed away under the tree.

Jake had scooted up the big maple tree as soon as the soldiers arrived. Now he was in the topmost branches where no one could see him, and he swayed there in the wind, a part of the branch, like a big bird hiding in its nest.

The captain sighed again so loud I could hear it, and then he walked in circles around my father, then bigger circles, maybe hoping he could change everything that was making him angry just by moving and moving some more. I knew the feeling.

In my early days in the castle after Eugenie and I had changed places, everything was so new and so tiring to remember and my whole world was topsy-turvy that some days only moving from place to place —long walks down the castle hallways —made me feel better. It was like the moving made sense of everything. Maybe that explained the captain's bigger and bigger circles.

Finally, with all our flowers gathered onto a wagon, he and his men left to go back toward the old couple's house. I wanted to run to the shortcut through the woods and hide and see what happened. But my father saw I was edging away and called me back. I glanced up into the maple tree and saw that Jake was gone. Somehow he made his way from tree to tree. I knew exactly where he was going.

Chapter Nine

Here's what Jake told me happened. I have tried to adjust all this and translate it from Jake talk. He only told parts of things, so what I know is really half of what Jake told me and half of me making up things to fill in.

We were in the barn, back behind the cow stalls where we could see if anyone came through the door. The barn was hushed with all the animals outside, only one owl now, and he was probably sleeping. I realized how fond I was of the leather and hay and even the manure smell, how fond I was of Jake and his excited talking style — what I had traded for the castle and tutors and silk dresses.

He told me he had been looking down on the whole thing. The King's men, the servants gathered around the edges with their empty baskets, a small wind waving the top branches above him and then in the path from the woods, the old woman and the old man were just standing there. They weren't moving, not saying anything, like pictures instead of real people. And, as they had before, the soldiers tried to enter the garden but as soon as they stepped in, they got confused, forgot what they were there for and finally stepped out again scratching their heads. Then the next group entered. Same thing.

Jake told me that the captain, after a short while, saw the old couple looking on. The captain immediately called for them to come. But they didn't move. Jake said they were not only not moving, but they seemed harder to see, for some reason. "It was as if the light was passing through them," Jake described it. "They faded, sort of. And I kept blinking because I thought I might be seeing things. You know, like you do sometimes late in the evening when you can't see things clearly. But this was bright sunlight. And they faded. Even got wavy like heat makes the road wavy sometimes and makes it look like water."

The captain kept shouting for them to come to him. Then he sent two soldiers after the old couple but Jake said the soldiers went down the path to fetch them, and when they got to the old couple, the fading got more and more until the two old people simply disappeared at the edge of the woods.

The captain stomped his foot in anger. He yelled at his men to chase the old people into the woods, but the soldiers just looked confused and then slowly went into the woods to get away from the shouting captain who was getting madder and madder by the second. He then tried to go into the garden himself. He clomped in with his shiny boots and stood in the middle with the same confused look on his face, but his feet kept on stomping up and down, up and down like a toy soldier going nowhere. Jake stomped his feet up and down joyfully in telling me this part.

Here Jake took a big breath. He said, "It was like everything had stopped except for the captain stomping his feet and not going anywhere. It was funny, like someone was telling a joke and then just stopped and left everyone in the joke…"

Jake pondered the rest of his sentence, thought hard about what should come after the word "joke." Then he sighed and looked up at the top of the big maple. Maybe the rest of the sentence was there. I smiled and waited. Jake began again.

"So, they all stopped, but I couldn't see why. The garden was still there. The soldiers and the captain and the people waiting with baskets were there, but nothing was happening. Stuck. That's what it was. Stuck."

And that seemed to settle it for him. He was satisfied with the word "stuck." He was quiet again, checking the treetops for whatever it was he thought was there. Well, he would know, of course. The treetops were his home. I always thought he only visited us here on the ground and then went back to the trees as easy as we might go home. He seemed now to be staying here with me just to be friendly. I know he'd scoot up the nearest tree if I turned to go. But his story about the captain and the old couple wasn't finished. At least for me it wasn't. And then we heard a loud noise. Maybe it was a cannon. It came from the woods near the old people's house.

Jake jumped straight up like a rabbit does in the spring. I should say he hopped. And before I knew it, he skittered up the tallest tree and looked out toward the woods.

"What do you see?" I called out to him. "Is it the King's men?" But my voice got lost in the wind, in the rustle of the leaves. I waited, knowing he'd come down when he was ready. And then the cannon boomed again. And again.

I heard Jake's voice through the rustle of the leaves. "They're shooting the garden."

And that was all the information he was going to give me. Maybe there was nothing more to tell. How do you shoot a garden? I could hear the answer to that echoing through the woods: over and over and over.

My parents came out and stood near the patch of stalks that had been our garden. I asked if I could go to the old people's house to see what was happening. I said I wouldn't go too close. I said I would be careful. I said I'd take Jake. My mother said, "Absolutely not. We have no idea what awful thing is going on there. And we will just have to wait to find out.

My father stood with his hands on his hips inspecting the ruin of our garden. It looked as if someone had tragically planted the wrong seeds and instead of flowers, only sticks had come up. I thought for a second that it was weirdly funny now that it was done. But I also knew enough not to share that with my family. Or with Eugenie when I would see her. She would not think there was one funny thing about this mess. After all, it was her flowers, her work, her care that had been taken from the garden and hauled off for the wedding of Arbuckle Beauregard the Third. The cannon sounded again and then was silent for a long time.

We went about our chores, my father with one eye on the direction of the soldiers, my mother making sure she could see me at all times. Jake kept to himself in the top of the tree. And soon, except for the garden of sticks, our life hummed right back to where it had been. But I knew the wedding final preparations were now in full swing. Soldiers and captains and servants were ranging through the kingdom collecting as many flowers as they could carry. Wagons full passed on the road, all headed for the castle. And soon the road itself was strewn with fallen flowers gathering dust with some crushed under the wheels of the next wagon in line, a sad train that seemed to never stop all day. All the spring color was flowing toward the wedding at the castle.

And the next day — the day before the wedding — the same sad train filled the road. And that afternoon, Eugenie appeared at the window in the barn where we lifted the hay into the loft. She *pssted*. Then again.

I pretended not to hear, of course. Then after pushing my hair back and adding a little wave to her, I slowly worked my way toward the barn.

The barn was cool inside with specks of light through every crevice and hole. Everything in there was serious and playful at the same time. The oiled leather, the order to the tools hanging on the wall, the sparrows cheeping in the rafters. Quiet cats appeared and disappeared while a slight rustling in the loft told me where Eugenie was. The playful part was how much the whole barn reminded me of a giant toy ready for fun. We had learned where it was safe to jump into the hay, where you could hide and pop out, where the most amazing tiny nests were hidden. Even the mice, the great joy of all the cats, had their place in the toy—at least until they ended up in the mouth of a cat, tail out one side, whiskers out the other.

As soon as I had climbed into the loft, carefully checking to see that father and mother were nowhere around, Eugenie popped out of the hay like a doll with stalks poking out of her hair, her eyes big as moons.

"I got away," she announced. "I saw what they did— what they tried to do—at the old couple's garden." And then in a rush, the whole story came out. "They shot a cannon into the garden and the cannon ball just slowly got smaller and thinner and then was gone. So they did it again. And again. And each time the same thing happened like there really wasn't a cannon ball in the first place. And even better, they never could find the old people, not in the woods or in the fields or anywhere!"

"But won't you get in trouble leaving the castle?" I asked.

She laughed. "No, no. Nobody in the castle is doing anything or watching anything except the wedding. People are everywhere and everybody is in a tizzy, running around and clucking to themselves like a thousand hens." She was delighted, I think, to be free again. She took a deep breath, inhaling the aroma of the barn. "Oh, I missed this. It smells like heaven to me."

"Also smells like manure," I added. "But I understand what you mean. Tell me what's happening at the castle."

Eugenie paused and thought. "Well, first of all, there is

---

the wedding—the flowers, the food, the silly bowing and eye-rolling and scheming about who sits next to whom. But after that, the new buzzing is all about one old couple who live in the woods—*our* old couple! How their flower garden has some powerful magic and even the strongest cannons could not break through that magic. The army generals want to know what it is so they can use it for the army. The priests want to know if it is from heaven or hell. And the poor King and Queen are worried that it could be the beginning of rebellion among the people. The wedding is taking a kind of second place to all these ways to be afraid. I laughed when I heard the first reports. The old couple, of course, were nothing to fear. But somehow everyone has managed to become more and more afraid anyway. I wanted to jump up and tell them how foolish they all were. But after the punishment for talking up at the Council meeting, I thought it better to keep my mouth shut this time. Be ignored for a while so I could get out of the castle."

She paused. We both listened for any stirrings in the barn below—Jake, my father or mother. We heard only the horses shifting feet and munching hay. The resident barn owl gave two hoots, and we both laughed. The two hoots were for us.

I asked, "But what will they do with the old couple?"

"Nothing! That's just it. They can't *do* anything because they can't find them. The soldiers left people at their house, but they didn't come back at night. Soldiers in the woods, all around the countryside, and they couldn't find a sign of the old ones. It was as if they rose up into the air and disappeared. Of course, there are sightings. I'd have been surprised if no one had *thought* they saw the old man limping through the market with his cane. *Thought* they saw the old woman for a second down an alleyway in town." Eugenie pulled a straw from her hair and looked at it. "I think they won't show up until after the wedding has taken place."

"Well, already the people are talking here in the village about how important it was that the flower garden couldn't be taken by the King's men," I added.

"I think I know where the old people are hiding," Eugenie announced grandly. "The soldiers can search the woods all they want and they will never see where they went. But I spent many hours in the woods collecting seed to grow in my garden. And I saw them one time, across a clearing, moving slowly in the sunlight at the edge of the woods. There was a giant oak tree there, one of the old ones left over from before they cut any trees in that forest. You know, one of those trees that look like an old face is hidden in the bark because of all the bumps and growths on it. Well, the old people were right next to it, I looked down at something running across my path, and when I looked up again, they were gone. Like they just melted into that tree. They were moving so slowly they couldn't have gone anywhere else. At the time, I thought they just stepped behind the giant tree, so I waited. And waited. Then finally, I walked across the clearing and then around the tree twice, all the time carefully watching for them, looking for the trail they would have made in the long grass. There was none."

"Could there have been a door in the tree," I asked. And then I felt a little foolish. She would have seen a door, of course. And I had been in those woods many time times with my father, looking for firewood. I had seen a number of the old trees Eugenie was talking about.

"Just the tree," she said, finally. "One big tree."

"And now what should we do?" I had some ideas, but I thought I'd let her go first.

"Alyssa, I have a feeling that the old couple have taken care of everything. But I think we should make sure. I have been thinking about this for a long time while locked in my room. And now I think we should both go to the wedding, both be there. Because whatever the old people have planned, it will occur at the wedding. You go as you, I'll go as me and meet all the important guests."

"But they won't let a farm girl in, will they? I won't be able to sneak in again while the wedding is going on. They'll be watching. And watching even more if they are worried about the old people's magic."

"It's not a problem," Eugenie said confidently. "Everyone is invited: villagers, farmers, even strangers passing through. I like to think my little speech changed their minds about the wedding being just for important people. Maybe not. But whatever changed their minds, the King pronounced that *everyone* would be invited: famous and noble, *gardeners*, everyone. Then no one could be unhappy." She lay back on the hay and chewed on a straw. "This is going to be good. Oh, yes. This is going to be excellent."

Chapter Ten

Eugenie went back to the castle my old secret way—through the woods instead of the road, along the path that wove in and out of the grasslands full of birds.

The wedding was the next day, and the king's men and lines of servants with baskets had collected every flower from every garden they could find. Not the old couple's though. After bringing in religious people and cannons and that angry captain of the guard to try to pry their flowers out of their beautiful garden, nothing worked, and they gave up. No one could find the old couple though they searched the entire woods.

All the kingdom was invited but not everyone could come. The farms far away at the border of the realm were just too distant, and the farmers and families couldn't leave their cows and other work too long. But our village and a few more nearby, all planned to go to the castle. As I was going home, a few families walked the road toward the wedding. I guess they planned to camp overnight and get good seats. But most of the travelling started early the next day.

I woke and looked out my window where clouds of dust hid the stream of travelers on the road. It looked like a long fuzzy snake with no head or tail winding toward the castle. My mother and father rounded up Jake, and I was given the job of making him presentable. I wasn't sure how well he would behave if he had to stay on the ground very long. But I did my best to dust him off, clean his hands, and do some kind of combing to his wild hair. My mother asked only that I make him look like a human being rather than a wild tree creature.

I stood back and admired my work. He was clean and his hair would stay plastered to his head at least as long as my mother's inspection. Then it would probably spring off in every direction as usual. I loved my brother, but he seemed made of different stuff than the rest of us: his need to be high in a tree, his strong nails for climbing like a squirrel, his delight in anything odd. I think the newness part is why he spent so much time in treetops, waving to and fro clinging to the thinnest branches. We all worried about him, but little by little we began to trust his antics. My mother just sighed and patted him on the head if he let her. My father believed that Jake would be a fine farmer after he grew big enough to work hard and love the land. And there was no question that Jake was brave, my father said about Jake's tree tricks. And you had to be brave to be a farmer. So it was settled.

My mother and father carried baskets with food (my mother said, in case there wasn't enough to eat at the wedding). "Okay, let's go," she said. "Bring the old blanket in case there are not enough chairs there. And water. We'll all need water to spend the day in the sun."

She seemed, like the rest of the village, excited about the wedding even though all had lost their flowers to decorate the tables. My father had said we would make up the money somehow. He didn't know exactly how. "Maybe pickles," he said, laughing. "Lots and lots of pickles. After all, the King's men didn't take the cucumbers."

My mother added, "They didn't take the cucumbers because they were too small to amount to anything when they came raiding." My mother, like Eugenie, was still mad about the flowers, and she wasn't going to stop being mad for a long time.

My father wagged a finger in the air as we set out. "But just for today, we're going to be happy to be part of this historic wedding that brings together two important families and keeps us peaceful. That's what I'm thinking about. All the important families coming together so there will be no war for a long, long time. If the cost of that peace is all the flowers in the world, well then, it's a small price to pay." Another finger wag and the subject of the stolen flowers was closed. But I knew that my mother and Eugenie still seethed inside. Flowers meant more to both of them than just plants. They both saw flowers as something delightful the earth gave us just for being alive. I understood their joy even if I found my own happiness elsewhere.

We made our way out our path toward the road to join in the dust and chatter headed toward the castle. As we passed the old couple's cottage and still beautiful flower garden, I stopped to take a stone from my shoe. "I'll catch up," I told my family.

But when I pulled my shoe off, there was no stone, though it certainly had felt like a stone. I poked around inside my shoe, but nothing was there. And then I heard a *psst*.

"Over here," came a small voice, so thin I thought at first it was the wind. "*Psst*. I have something for you. Listen carefully." The old woman was kneeling at the edge of her garden and in her hand was a small watering can, a smaller version of the big, empty one we had seen her using on her plants.

The little can had nothing in it. I shook it. She said quickly, "Don't worry. It's full. Take this with you and— now listen carefully—water only the flowers that will be on the tables for the villagers. Don't water any others. Just tip the can for a few seconds into the vases of all the flowers around the outside edge of the wedding. Do you understand?" Her voice was even more like the wind than when she had begun. "Now put your shoe on and catch up. Hide the watering can."

I bent to put my shoe on and when I looked up, she was gone. Maybe she went into the garden, but I couldn't see her anywhere. I hurried to catch up to my family after I tucked the small watering can away in my dress-up apron.

As we walked along I kept thinking: what just happened? Should I tell my mother and father? Should I ask Jake if he saw anything? He was always seeing what I couldn't. Should I tell Eugenie what the old woman had asked me to do? I decided that if I could, I would tell Eugenie, but that might be very difficult.

She would be greeting every ancient aunt and uncle and every famous family and friend of the castle. Her job would be to make sure every family story got repeated, every cousin's cheek kissed. Though I loved the castle life, the classes and duties, I was never really fond of the empty smiling and waving a princess had to do. I did it—would keep doing it—but just so I could get to the good part of being a princess.

The dust on the road covered my shoes, seemed to seek out and settle in Jake's hair, and made little kids cough, but didn't dampen the spirit of the people as we made our way to the castle. I felt for the watering can in my pocket. It was like a secret and a puzzle at the same time. I would, of course, try to do as the old woman said. I thought I would probably feel a little foolish pouring nothing out of the can into the vases of flowers. And if someone saw me? Then what? "What do you think you're doing there?" they would say. "Stop it, you...you...girl!" But if I was careful, maybe I could avoid that mess. I'd just slip along watering nothing into vases just as if it made sense. Poof, went the dusty road with each step. Poof. Poof. Maybe I should try watering the dust, I thought.

As we got closer to the castle, the dust stopped. The palace people had paved the road with shiny new cobbles. Far away at the edge of the castle wall, were the places set for the important people. Tables set in rings, I knew, so that the right people sat next to the other right people. And talked. They would have to talk. The flowers were thickest there as if the tables and chairs poked out of huge bouquets of bright yellows and reds, the fine and pale pastels with wisps of blue for accents. At the outside tables where the villagers were being shown their places, there were many fewer flowers, but on each table there were vases just as the old woman said there would be. And in each vase enough flowers to look like a celebration. It would take some work, but I could easily move around and do my secret watering. I couldn't wait to see what would happen. The instructions had been so quick and so like the wind, that I wasn't exactly sure what I'd heard. But I knew the watering part. The pretend watering part.

Eugenie stood shifting from foot to foot as a long line moved slowly past her. She spoke to this one, then to that one and nodded and smiled. I couldn't hear what she was saying, but I knew it had to be all the things I couldn't have said: how is cousin James? Oh, were they married last year? That fine dog you had, he must be old by now. She knew all the little princess things to say; and I also knew she was hating this part but doing it well so she could get back to her garden.

I moved through the crowd watching the important people greeting each other. If Eugenie saw me, she didn't make any sign. I knew I wanted to tell her what the old woman had asked of me. She would have an opinion. The entire crowd smelled like flowers. And from a little hill I could see everyone had worn their brightest and best clothes. The day was turning out like all the holidays rolled together and then mixed with a fine summer day.

My parents were keeping a close watch on Jake, who had a tendency to wander away to some high place. During market day last year, they found him on a rooftop squatting and just watching the sellers below. Once they found him high up a cliff with some young goats hopping between ledges. So now they kept him close by.

On the other hand, I was old enough to wander in the crowds and still be expected to find my way back to my family at the proper time. I felt not only grown up, but also double, like there were two of me circling on both sides of the wedding—among the notables and among the folk.

Eugenie had the hard part. Her feet must have been aching from standing. I could see her shifting feet in those tight, uncomfortable princess shoes. And the smiling part must have become tiresome very quickly. From where I watched, her smile looked like a picture of a smile drawn on her face, always the same, only her lips moving. I knew she was bringing great peace and many fine connections among the important families. After all, that was what this whole wedding was about.

But, yikes! So, I was happy with my freedom for the moment, and I used that freedom to move from table to table with my little watering can pretending to water each vase of flowers. I heard one woman say, "Isn't that sweet. She's keeping the flowers fresh with that tiny sprinkling can. Such a good girl." And I moved on.

From the castle walls flew flags of all the families with all their crests and bright colors. Arbuckle Pemberton the Third, now the center of great celebration, had been, not too long ago, considered a silly person with no future. Now he and his bride had become the center of a grand event that would become part of songs and stories forever.

Trumpets sounded. And I thought of all the stolen flowers sacrificed to make this event look joyous.

I made my way from table to table nodding and smiling with my watering can. I was patted on the head four times, on the shoulder three times, and complimented on my good posture once. I think some of those who looked closely and saw that no water came from my can might have thought I was a silly girl just pretending. But most people only nodded and smiled as I "watered" their vases.

The trumpets sounded again and hundreds of white doves were let loose from the castle walls. They flew together over the crowd and then back to the wall where they had been trained to return. Every ten minutes or so they would be let out again, darken the sun for a few seconds and fly back to their cages. Then more trumpets and everyone grew quiet.

Finally, Eugenie could sit down. I saw her move to the front of the large stage and take her princess place. Cousins and uncles and aunts followed. Then the dignitaries from close by and far off all were seated. Trumpets again. Doves again. I hurried with my watering because I had many tables to go, and I could guess the ceremony would start as soon as everyone was seated. Strangely the watering can, tiny though it was, felt heavier and heavier as I finished up. It seemed it was somehow filling up from the flowers instead of emptying into the vases. At the end I had to use two hands to lift it for the last row of vases. Then I was done. I felt a little disappointed that nothing had happened. All the flowers looked the same after my watering. Oh well, I tucked the can into my apron and went to find my family.

I kept thinking how much these flowers would cost in the village market. I could picture them in the stall of a friend's mother who would always throw in a small bouquet free if you bought flowers from her. She'd laugh and then make up someone's name who should receive the bouquet from you. "For your Aunt Mary," she'd say, or "for your boyfriend." The flowers from her garden brought the money she used for Christmas presents or to buy cloth and leather for everyday clothes for her children. These were her flowers and the flowers of many other careful gardeners.

The actual wedding began just as I returned to my family. Jake was not able to sit in a chair. He climbed up the back, then under and finally sat on his legs as mother scowled him into some kind of sitting. Mother and father seemed pleased to be surrounded by so much excitement as if they had joined up with all the others now in the happiness together. I couldn't get over the great flower robbery, but I kept a happy face just to join in. Eugenie, far away on the stage, sat with her hands folded looking like a princess. I wondered how she felt about the whole business as she looked out over these thousands of flowers shouting out wedding-day joy in a rainbow of bright colors.

The wedding itself went on for a long time, as you might expect. There had to be blessings and more flowers. There were songs. The doves again. More trumpets. And finally, cheering from everyone, famous and important and farmers alike. My favorite part was the long rolls of cloth made into a kind of portable ceiling for the happy bride and groom. The bride's dress was white and covered in some kind of sparkles so that when she walked in and out of the light and shade made by the rolls of cloth, she seemed to float at Arbuckle's side and then suddenly light up.

But the wedding was just the beginning of a long, long day.

Next came the ceremonies featuring the most important

families, a kind of parade of what looked like some very old people and some just slightly old people. And then the younger ones went on parade. The bride and groom were long gone, and we all watched the bright dresses and uniforms traipsing up and down. Jake fidgeted. Eugenie marched in the procession when her time came. I knew that all the while she was really longing to get her hands back in the dirt of her garden.

And then the eating. Roasts and chickens and fowl of all sorts streamed out from the castle in an endless parade—a finer parade than the notables, everyone agreed. After the royals were served, all the rest were fed. I kept wondering whose garden got raided for the vegetables, whose family will go hungry? The eating went on until nearly sundown. Trumpets announced the final ceremony and blessing of all.

Then it happened.

A little at a time at first, like the beginning of a gentle rain. Then more and more. All the flowers on the villagers' tables began to rain money. It seemed the flower petals melted into coins that rained onto the tables. Then the raining became a storm of coins flowing from each vase. The people gasped at first. Then they began to collect coins in pockets and furled aprons. All the flowers I had watered with my tiny watering can, but not the royal flowers, became coins.

I could hear whispers that the King and Queen must have found this way to pay the people for their flowers. But all of us could see that they, and all the others whose flowers had not become money, were just as surprised as we were.

But all the guests at the people's tables had money by the time all the petals from all the vases had changed into coins.

Everyone looked at each other in amazement. Then the explanations began.

"The priests must have done it with magic."

"The old ones, the star and moon priests, they certainly had a hand in this."

"Maybe the King and Queen and all the families got together..."

"No. No. Look at them. They can't believe it either. Look, some of them are emptying out their flower vases to see if there is money in them."

And there they were. Several old men were dumping out the royal flowers looking for more wealth to add to their own. But all they found were wilting flowers and warm water. And all they made was a mess on the fine table cloths. Only the villagers' tables sprouted coins.

I knew why and how. I patted the watering can in my apron and smiled to myself. Then I helped mother and father collect our share of the money, and then we helped others collect theirs.

By the time we were all on the road toward home, pockets full, bellies full, I could hear around us that most people thought the magic had come from the castle somehow, some way. After all, the castle was where all the power was kept. So certainly that power must be responsible for the great transformation of flowers into money. It was settled. By the time we left the highway for our farm, it was getting dark. And as we passed near the old couple's garden, I could barely see the path, but their garden was almost invisible in the failing light. What I could see was that the little light we had left from the day seemed to go right through the flower petals and out the other side. And one other thing, though I couldn't be sure because of the twilight. The old couple's house seemed abandoned, the windows like closed eyes of a sleeper. The door was hanging crooked. It looked as if no one had lived there in a very long time. I pointed it out to father, but he was carrying Jake by this point and wanted to hurry down the path toward home. Mother peered where I pointed but confessed she couldn't see very well.

Eugenie and I waited for three days before we tried to switch back. It turned out that she still had a number of duties involving old aunts and uncles, and she had to finish these before getting back to her garden. The talk of the castle was, of course, the flowers that had changed into money. Eugenie said that the flowers *always were* money, and so she wasn't the least bit surprised. And then she laughed our laugh. I, of course, told her about my little watering can. And we both laughed our laugh again.

But the rumor at the castle was that Arbuckle Pemberton the Third had made the transformation take place in honor of his wedding. After all, hadn't he saved the kingdom from the bad water? Hadn't he been the hero once before? Of course, it must have been his doing. And Arbuckle himself never denied it. So in time it would come to be believed as true.

Eugenie and I just laughed our laughs and went back to being who we really were—me to the castle, Eugenie to her farm garden.

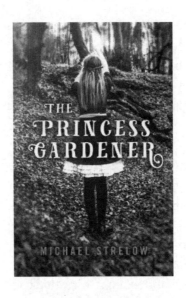

The Princess Gardener
Michael Strelow

The Princess Gardener is the story of a young girl who found herself a princess by accident of birth. What she really wants is outside the castle in the gardens: dirty hands, making things grow, feeling the seasons along with the plants she tends. But castle duties call more and more often, and her parents insist she learn what she calls "the princess business." She reluctantly curtseys and bows and smiles her way through the empty rituals of the kingdom, but every day she longs for the smell of the earth and the joys of gardening. One day, she finds an opportunity to switch lives with a young farm girl who is her exact likeness. Despite each girl finding what she always wanted, both their lives get very complicated very quickly...

(Our Street Books: 978-1-78535-674-2)

**OUR STREET
BOOKS**

Our Street Books

JUVENILE FICTION, NON-FICTION, PARENTING

Our Street Books are for children of all ages, delivering a potent mix of fantastic, rip-roaring adventure and fantasy stories to excite the imagination; spiritual fiction to help the mind and the heart; humorous stories to make the funny bone grow; historical tales to evolve interest; and all manner of subjects that stretch imagination, grab attention, inform, inspire and keep the pages turning. Our subjects include Non-fiction and Fiction, Fantasy and Science Fiction, Religious, Spiritual, Historical, Adventure, Social Issues, Humour, Folk Tales and more.

If you have enjoyed this book, why not tell other readers by posting a review on your preferred book site.

Recent bestsellers from Our Street Books are:

Relax Kids: Aladdin's Magic Carpet
Marneta Viegas
Let Snow White, the Wizard of Oz and other fairytale characters
show you and your child how to meditate and relax. Meditations
for young children aged 5 and up.
Paperback: 978-1-78279-869-9 Hardcover: 978-1-90381-666-0

Wonderful Earth
An interactive book for hours of fun learning
Mick Inkpen, Nick Butterworth
An interactive Creation story: Lift the flap, turn the wheel, look in
the mirror, and more.
Hardcover: 978-1-84694-314-0

Boring Bible: Super Son Series 1
Andy Robb
Find out about angels, sin and the Super Son of God.
Paperback: 978-1-84694-386-7

Jonah and the Last Great Dragon
Legend of the Heart Eaters
M.E. Holley
When legendary creatures invade our world, only dragon-fire can
destroy them; and Jonah alone can control the Great Dragon.
Paperback: 978-1-78099-541-0 ebook: 978-1-78099-542-7

Little Prayers Series: Classic Children's Prayers
Alan and Linda Parry
Traditional prayers told by your child's favourite creatures.
Hardcover: 978-1-84694-449-9

Magnificent Me, Magnificent You The Grand Canyon
Dawattie Basdeo, Angela Cutler
A treasure filled story of discovery with a range of inspiring fun exercises, activities, songs and games for children aged 6 to 11.
Paperback: 978-1-78279-819-4

Q is for Question
An ABC of Philosophy
Tiffany Poirier
An illustrated non-fiction philosophy book to help children aged 8 to 11 discover, debate and articulate thought-provoking, open-ended questions about existence, free will and happiness.
Hardcover: 978-1-84694-183-2

Relax Kids: How to be Happy
52 positive activities for children
Marneta Viegas
Fun activities to bring the family together.
Paperback: 978-1-78279-162-1

Rise of the Shadow Stealers
The Firebird Chronicles
Daniel Ingram-Brown
Memories are going missing. Can Fletcher and Scoop unearth their own lost history and save the Storyteller's treasure from the shadows?
Paperback: 978-1-78099-694-3 ebook: 978-1-78099-693-6

Readers of ebooks can buy or view any of these bestsellers by clicking on the live link in the title. Most titles are published in paperback and as an ebook. Paperbacks are available in traditional bookshops. Both print and ebook formats are available online.

Find more titles and sign up to our readers' newsletter at
http://www.johnhuntpublishing.com/children-and-young-adult
Follow us on Facebook at https://www.facebook.com/JHPChildren
and Twitter at https://twitter.com/JHPChildren